MW01118296

Sharpe Note: Sour Grapes of Wrath

Maycroft Mysteries, Volume 7

Lisa B. Thomas

Published by Lisa B. Thomas, 2019.

SHARPE NOTE

Copyright © 2018 Lisa B. Thomas

Cozy Stuff and Such, LLC

Chapter 1

IT NEVER OCCURRED TO Deena Sharpe that she would be attending two funerals in one month or that she'd be changing jobs again so soon. In fact, what weighed heaviest on her mind that fateful day in early February was whether she should wear flats or heels.

Gary stared in the dresser mirror adjusting the knot on his fancy designer necktie. "I'm sorry we have to spend our anniversary this way." Deena had given him that tie last year for their anniversary, and it was his favorite. "I'll make it up to you."

Deena stroked mascara onto her eyelashes. "No worries. It's not like you knew in advance we'd be attending a funeral today. Tragedy has its own calendar."

"Ah, very wise indeed. Did you read that in a fortune cookie?"

"No, it's just one of the many brilliant things that pop into your wife's head. You should expect that after being married *thirty*..." Deena stopped to do the mental math needed to determine which anniversary they were celebrating.

"It's thirty-six," Gary said quickly.

"Oh, that's right." She put on some lip gloss and closed her makeup drawer. "According to Hallmark, it's the year you're supposed to give antiques."

"That's appropriate since you're an antique dealer." Gary pointed down the hall toward the guest room. "I'll just go in there and grab one of those 'treasures' that still hasn't made it out to your booth at the antiques mall and wrap it up for you."

"Very funny. You know it has only been a few weeks since Sandra came back to the thrift store after her maternity leave. I'll have more time now that I'm not covering for her."

"I'm surprised there's anything left at the thrift store to sell. Don't think I didn't notice all those bags you've been bringing home."

Deena leaned over and pecked his cheek. "Let's get back to your feeling guilty about dragging me to a memorial service for a man I barely knew. And on our anniversary, no less."

Gary let out a sigh. "Drew Granger. I know he was a client, but I also considered him a friend. It's so hard to believe he killed himself. It seemed like he had everything going for him. A successful business, a great house, a loving wife."

Deena put on her coat and tried to stay upright in her funeral shoes—black heels that seemed harder to walk in every time she wore them. She made a mental note to shop for a more comfortable pair the next time she was out.

As they got in Gary's red sports car—a midlife-crisis purchase from a few years back—Deena thought about the list her husband had just rattled off. "I noticed you mention a 'successful business' before a 'loving wife.' Is that how you prioritize your life?"

Gary rolled his eyes. "Of course not. My list starts with this car."

Deena gave him a playful punch on the arm. "By the way, how do you know that his wife was loving? Maybe they had a bad marriage and that led to his depression."

"I guess it's because he always seemed to make a point of mentioning Allison when we talked about his finances. He included her name in all the paperwork involving the vineyard, even though the business was only his."

As they drove to the funeral home, Deena thought about the man they would soon be memorializing. It had been in all the major newspapers, even dominated the newscasts for a good two days, but as the restless public hungered for their next meal, the story of Andrew Granger's suicide was soon discarded like old trash.

Except in Maycroft.

The Grangers were a well-to-do family originally from Lubbock. The family patriarch, Edward Granger, Sr., had made his fortune in West Texas oil. Not quite the Beverly Hillbillies, the family moved east to Dallas where Edward, Jr., parlayed his family's fortune into millions. They'd rubbed elbows with politicians and the wealthy Southern elite.

However, bad investments in the nineties saw the family fortune fritter away as they tried to keep up appearances. Edward's wife reportedly died of a weak heart, although some suspected suicide. The grieving widower found God then and invested his remaining money into a struggling vineyard just outside Maycroft in East Texas. His business motto became "Granger's Grapes: God's Fruit."

As the vines matured, so did his two children, Edwina and Andrew, who both joined the family business and were around when their signature wine won its first major award.

Last week when Andrew Granger's death was determined to be a suicide, the whispers began again as folks wondered if he'd inherited his mama's "weak heart."

The chapel of Mortimer's Funeral Home was sparsely filled as happens when the people who come to mourn the deceased don't really know each other. Gary and Deena sat near the middle on the opposite side of Drew's widow. She was decked out in a black dress with small white polka dots. Deena couldn't help thinking they reminded her of champagne bubbles.

Not surprisingly, several of the sprays of flowers on the front table contained violets and other seasonal purple flowers. The ornate bronze urn sat on a table decorated with baskets of ivy and lush blue and purple grapes. It was a fitting tribute for a man who owned a vineyard.

After settling into their spot, Deena looked around for people she might know. A few faces seemed familiar, but none of Deena's friends were there. Drew and his wife were younger than Deena and Gary. Allison was a teller at the bank, but Deena had never really talked to her much.

The service followed the usual format: organ music, favorite hymns, a semi-generic sermon by the pastor, and lots of prayers.

The part Deena dreaded was up next as the pastor called for friends and family to pay tribute to the man whose picture stared back at them. This is where some people had the need to share stories about inside jokes they had with the deceased and others fell into a puddle of tears. Both were uncomfortable to witness.

A hush fell over the crowd as those in attendance waited to see who would get up first. A few people seemed as though they were tempted to stand but thought better of it and sat back. Others shook their heads awkwardly as husbands or wives prodded them to get up and say something. Finally, one man stood and made his way to the front as an audible sigh of relief rose from the pews.

Deena whispered to Gary, "Who is that? He looks familiar."

"Lonnie Fisher," Gary said, offering no other information.

The man shook hands with the pastor and cleared his throat before bending toward the microphone on the podium. He was a small man, sharply dressed in a gray suit with a lavender shirt and violet tie. His receding hairline was offset by a well-manicured beard. He kept his eyes low as he spoke.

"As many of you know, Drew and I were best friends. In fact, we were more like family than friends. I've been with Drew at the vineyard for almost ten years, and in those ten years, I grew to love the man." He glanced at the widow. "I know we'll all miss Drew for his kind heart and gentle spirit. Hopefully, he's in a better place now. May he rest in peace."

"Amen," the pastor said as Lonnie walked back to his seat. "Who would like to be next?" He looked around and then back to the row where Allison sat with several family members.

Allison shook her head.

That poor woman, Deena thought. Suicide was such a tragedy for those left behind. Less grizzly than murder, more salacious than a car accident, a suicide left people to wonder and speculate the what-ifs about the deceased.

The pastor proceeded to offer up a closing prayer and then invited loved ones to a reception at the Granger home.

Gary had already told Deena they would be attending the reception. He was always particular about those types of occasions. He thought failing to go to the reception after a funeral was like a guest coming to dinner and getting up to leave before the main course. He got his sense of duty from Miss Manners herself—his mother, Sylvia.

They all waited as the family filed out. Deena wondered which ones were Grangers and which ones were on Allison's side of the family. The two blondes were obviously sisters or cousins of Allison's. She wasn't sure about the others.

As she watched the family walk by, Deena imagined herself in Allison's position. What if something happened to Gary? Would she be able to hold up as well as Allison seemed to be? The answer was simple: absolutely not. Gary was her rock. Her compass. Her true north. She often told him that if he died before her, she'd never forgive him.

And she meant it.

Just as Allison was passing the back row, an older man stood up and stepped in front of her. Deena couldn't see Allison's face, but she heard her say, "I'm surprised you came."

The man flashed her a wry smile. "Just wanted to make sure he was good and dead."

Chapter 2

THE GRANGERS LIVED in one of the older neighborhoods in town, where the yards were large and well-manicured and the houses were set back from the street. Their house had been updated and stuck out among the others as a diamond in the rough.

It was kind of creepy having the reception at the Grangers' house, considering the fact that Drew had shot himself in the couple's bed. That was a tidbit of information Deena had learned from her friend Dan Carson, news editor for the *Northeast Texas Tribune*. Sometimes it paid to have friends in high-*ish* places. Gary made Deena promise not to sneak off for a peek inside the bedroom. She had crossed her fingers and made a vague sound that Gary might have interpreted as "okay."

Neither Gary nor Deena recognized the creepy man who had practically accosted Allison as she had left the funeral chapel. Deena was determined to talk to him if he showed up at the reception. Gary rationalized that he might be a distant relative jealous of Drew's fortune and success.

The food was catered by a company out of Dallas, and Deena loaded up her plate with potato salad and barbequed brisket while eyeing the chocolate meringue pie for dessert. She followed Gary to a table where Lonnie Fisher, cradling a glass of wine, sat with a few other men. Gary offered condolences and they proceeded with the introductions. As it turned out, Lonnie was the production manager at the vineyard, and the two other men worked for him.

"Deena," Gary said, "I'm sure you remember meeting Lonnie last summer when we visited the winery. He joined us on the personal tour with Drew."

Nothing like putting her on the spot. She smiled and said, "Of course. And I'm so sorry for your loss."

Lonnie stared into his glass of wine as though Drew's picture were floating inside. "Thank you." He fidgeted with a gold ring on his right hand.

Deena was surprised Lonnie was single, being that he was nice looking, well dressed, and had a good job. He was a triple threat in her book. He wasn't eating. That's probably how he kept his trim physique.

No one said much until Gary spoke up. "Do you know what's going to happen to the business now that Drew is gone? Will Allison get involved or does she plan to sell it?"

"Sell it?" Lonnie bolted upright and stared at Gary as though the notion were unthinkable. He looked as though he might be sick. Not only had he lost his best friend, but he had also lost his employer.

"Oh, Gary," Deena said quickly, "no one wants to talk business now. Have you tried the brisket? It's really moist."

Gary apologized and turned his attention to his plate.

When everyone sat quietly for an uncomfortable amount of time, Deena looked back at Lonnie and asked, "So how did you and Drew meet?" After she asked the question, she realized it sounded like something you'd ask a newly engaged couple.

Regardless, Lonnie's eyes lit up. "Actually, it was almost ten years ago. I saw an ad online looking for a manager for a small rural company. It didn't say what kind of company. I was living in Dallas at the time and had just gotten out of a bad relationship. I was ready for a change. Also, you know how Dallas traffic is." He smiled and took a sip of tea.

"Terrible," Deena said and nodded.

"The idea of living in the country was tempting, so I applied. When I found out the job was at a winery, I was thrilled. My grandparents moved here from Italy, so we're wine drinkers from way back. In fact, I was told Pavarotti might be a sixth cousin."

"Isn't he that old race car driver?" one of the other men asked.

"No, that's Mario Andretti," Gary said.

"Then who's this Pavarotti?"

Lonnie snorted in frustration. "He's just the greatest tenor of all time, that's all." He fell silent again.

Deena took that as her cue to scope out the dessert table again. As luck would have it, an elderly woman holding a cane was just picking up the last piece of pie. Deena pictured herself grabbing the cane, whacking the old lady, and making a run for it with the pie.

"We're cutting some more," a girl with the catering staff said. "It will be just a few minutes."

Deena smiled and opted to hang out near the table just in case there was another rush on dessert. The mystery man from the funeral was nowhere in sight. But standing near her was Allison Granger in her champagne-bubble frock and high heels. Women like her made it look easy. She probably didn't have to stand on her feet all day at the bank like Deena did when she was a teacher. Consequently, Deena's feet were better suited for flats than heels.

Allison was talking to a man in a brown sports coat who had loosened his tie. Judging by Allison's expression and crossed arms, she didn't appear too happy with the guy. Deena inched closer.

"No, I haven't talked to her in years," Brown Suit said. "I assumed Drew was still in touch."

"Lord, no," Allison said. "Apparently, when they had their falling-out with their father, Drew just wrote his sister off. He never would tell me what happened between them, and I never asked. That's why I didn't bother to track her down to tell her that Drew was gone."

"So, you don't know what happened between her and the family?" he asked.

"No clue," Allison said. "I've never even met her. I mean, she's your wife, don't you know where she is?"

He shuffled his feet. "Like I said, she and I split right after she quit the business. I only found out about Drew's death through seeing it in the newspaper."

Allison nodded and mumbled, "Uh-huh." She looked around as though she wanted an excuse to get away.

Deena wanted to rescue her from what appeared to be an uncomfortable conversation, so she walked over and shot out her hand to Allison. "Hi, I'm Deena Sharpe, Gary's wife."

Allison, looking relieved, reached out and returned the shake. "Thank you so much for coming. But will you excuse me? There's someone I need to speak to." She walked off toward the hallway where a uniformed police officer stood. Deena recognized him as Officer Larry Linndorf.

"Say, aren't you that murder-solving lady I read about in the local papers?" Brown Suit asked. "I remember thinking, 'That Deena Sharpe must be really sharp!'"

She offered up a half smile at the lame joke she'd heard numerous times. "That's me. Actually, I'm an investigator for a law firm."

"Like a PI?"

"Sort of." Not wanting to explain that she was not a licensed private detective, but instead worked on a contract basis with Ian Davis, she looked for her own excuse to get away.

Luckily, the caterer came out of the kitchen with a tray full of desserts.

"Oh look. It's pie," she said. Grabbing two pieces, she excused herself and scooted past the man to make her way back to Gary.

"Thanks, hon, but you know I don't like meringue," Gary said as she set the plate in front of him.

"Yeah, I know." She pulled his plate closer and dug her fork into the creamy slice of heaven. The pie made it almost worth being dragged there on her anniversary.

As she expected, the conversation at the table turned to sports. Lonnie got up and joined another group of mourners while Gary and the winery employees talked about basketball. After finishing her pie and eating just the meringue off Gary's, she got up to find the restroom. If she just happened to open the door to the master bedroom, it would practically be an accident.

A portrait of Allison in her wedding gown hung in the hall-way. She looked beautiful in her beaded dress and long train. Gary had said the couple had no children. Deena thought Allison would have no trouble finding another man to spend the rest of her life with.

The hallway looked like the typical three-bedroom arrangement and all the doors were closed. Guessing the first door on the left led to a guest bedroom, Deena skipped it and headed for the second, thinking that it could be the master or possibly a second guest room. She turned the knob and opened the door to find Officer Linndorf talking to Allison. "Excuse me," she said and quickly closed it.

Just then a woman walked out of the bathroom on the other side of the hall. Deena ducked inside and locked the door behind her. Not only was she embarrassed, but she didn't even get a good look at the bedroom. She stared in the mirror and took a few deep breaths, trying to slow down her heart rate.

Could the police really be questioning poor Allison at her husband's funeral reception? If so, she was going to have a word with Detective Guttman. That just wasn't right. Allison had looked upset and Linndorf was standing there with his hands on his gun belt like the police do when they want to look tough or when they're preparing to draw a weapon.

Deena planned how she'd escape this situation without having to face Allison again. She texted Gary, saying she would be coming out of the bathroom in one minute and that they needed to leave right away. She got a return message saying "Ok" and then put her ear to the door. She didn't hear any voices or footsteps and figured the coast was clear. She slowly opened the door and hurried to her waiting husband.

When they got outside, he asked, "Are you okay? Did all that pie make you sick?"

She walked ahead of him to the car. When they got inside, she let out a sigh of relief. "I'm fine, I was just ready to go."

Gary started up the car. "But I didn't even get a chance to speak to Allison."

"I spoke to her for both of us," Deena said as she put on her seat belt. "Don't worry. I'm sure I made an impression on her."

Chapter 3

A FEW DAYS LATER DEENA got a call from her boss's new secretary, Paulette. She said a woman who wouldn't give her name wanted an appointment to meet with her.

"With me?" Deena asked. "Are you sure she wanted to meet with me and not with Ian?"

"She asked for you by name. Do you want me to set it up?"

"Sure," Deena said, wondering who in the world would ask for her directly.

The more she thought about it, the more certain Deena felt that it was likely someone trying to sell her life insurance or to get her to sign up for some pyramid scheme. Either way, Deena was excited to get back to the office. Since she had been working at the thrift store after Sandra and Ian's baby was born, she was itching for a new assignment. Hopefully, Ian would have some cases that required her special investigative talents. She didn't care if it was trailing a cheating husband or spying on a crooked employee, she was just ready to do something useful.

When she pulled up to the restored Victorian house that served as Ian Davis's law office, she noticed a woman sitting out front in her car talking on her phone. Deena wondered if this was the woman with whom she had an appointment. She didn't want to stare, so she went inside and greeted Paulette. Deena had only met her once before.

Paulette had a wide, welcoming smile. "How are you, Mrs. Sharpe? Is there anything I can get you?" She grabbed Deena's coat to hang it on the hall tree.

"First of all, please call me Deena. And second, I can manage my own coat."

"I'm sorry, *Mrs....* I mean, Deena. I'm still getting used to working in a real office. When Mr. Davis gave me this job so I could meet the terms of my probation, I started watching different TV shows to see how I was supposed to behave. I've been practicing."

Deena smiled. "Relax. I'm sure you'll do fine. Do you know if that woman sitting out there in her car is waiting for me?"

Paulette went to the large front window and looked out. "I don't know. I don't recognize her though."

"Well, I'll be in my office. Just ring me when she gets here."

"Yes, ma'am," Paulette said, taking her seat back behind the desk.

Deena looked around her small office. Except for a thin layer of dust on her desk, everything looked as she had left it. She felt right at home. After all, Sandra wasn't just the boss's wife, she was Deena's best friend. In fact, she and Gary were baby Sylvia's godparents.

Ugh. She still had a hard time accepting that the Davises gave their baby the same name as Deena's mother-in-law. She hoped baby Sylvia wouldn't grow up to be a snooty busybody.

The phone rang.

"Ms. Deena, your appointment lady is here. I can't tell you her name because she won't give it to me."

"That's fine," Deena said. "Let her know I'll be right out."

Note to self: Talk to Paulette about her phone etiquette. Deena took an old red scarf that had been hanging in her office and wiped off the desktop before straightening her jacket and walking out to greet the mystery woman.

"Hi, I'm Deena Sharpe." She reached out her hand.

The petite brunette did the fingertip shake and simply said, "Hi."

That was usually the sign of an insecure person or a genteel Southerner. From her appearance, the woman could be either. She wore a cheap polyester dress that was a size too large and had on loafers in serious need of a good polish. Her mousy-brown hair was pulled back in a ponytail—not the high-up, cutesy kind, but the low, lying on her neck kind. With no makeup and eyeglasses that made her look older than she probably was, all Deena could think of was an elementary school librarian in serious need of a makeover.

Deena led the woman down the hall. She really wasn't used to meeting with clients in her own office; they usually met in Ian's office or in the small conference room.

The woman took the chair across from Deena's desk and clutched her handbag in her lap.

"So, what can I do for you?" Deena asked. "But before you say anything, I want to make it clear that I'm not a lawyer."

"Oh, I know that, Mrs. Sharpe. You're the reason I'm here. My name is Edwina Granger, and I want to hire you to catch the person who killed my brother. And, I know who did it."

Deena was totally caught off guard. "Are you talking about Drew Granger?"

"Yes, ma'am. I know that the Maycroft police said he killed himself, but I think he was murdered."

"I see. So you've talked to the police."

"No, ma'am. I read about it in the newspapers."

There was a slight twang in her voice, and she sat pencil straight as though she were applying for a job. Except for the posture, nothing about her said "upper-class heir of the Granger fortune." If she were indeed on the Granger family tree, her branch must have broken and fallen off.

Deena realized she should be taking notes and fumbled in the desk drawer for paper and pen while she collected her thoughts. Not being a licensed private detective, she couldn't take the case on her own. Perhaps the woman wanted to hire the law firm. Either way, Deena needed to hear her out. She was a Granger, after all. "Let's start at the beginning. You say your name is Edwina Granger." Deena wrote it down. "And you state that Drew—"

"Andrew..." Edwina corrected.

"*Andrew* Granger was your brother."

Could this be the sister she overheard Allison talking about at the reception? If so, the woman hadn't been in touch with her brother for years. "Are you Andrew Granger's only sister?"

"Yes, ma'am. And he's my only brother."

Ah-ha. The estranged sister was back in town to make trouble. To Edwina she said, "What exactly was your relationship like with your brother before he died?"

"Oh, we were close. We talked at least once a week."

Her answer came quick, almost as if rehearsed. "Really? In person or on the phone?"

"On the phone. I don't live around here."

None of this jived with what Allison had told Brown Suit. She had said Drew had cut all ties with his sister. Perhaps they kept up their relationship in secret. But why?

"Where do you live?" Deena poised her pen over the notepad ready to write down the address.

"Not in Texas. I live in another state."

That narrowed it down to forty-nine. "Um, could you tell me which one?"

"No," Edwina said and squeezed the patent leather handbag tighter in her lap. "Not until I know if you are going to help me."

Deena was used to questioning hostile witnesses, but usually they were on the other side of the case. Potential clients were generally more forthcoming than this.

"Well, then can you tell me when you last spoke to your brother?"

"It was Wednesday, the day before he was murdered." She said it with the same emotion a person would use when placing their order at a McDonald's drive-thru.

"And how was your brother when you talked to him?"

"Fine."

"Fine," Deena repeated. "What did you two talk about? Did he say if he was worried about anything? Did he seem upset?"

"No. He was fine."

"Got it. *Fine.*" Deena thumped her pen on the legal pad.

"Look, I know I may sound like a crazy person, but I'm telling the truth. My brother wasn't the type to take his own life. He was a strong man."

Deena nodded and proceeded slowly. "Like you, I too have read about your brother's death in the newspaper. It was a shock to everyone here as I'm sure it was for you. From what I read, a neighbor heard a noise and called the police. When they got there, he had a gun next to him and was...gone."

Edwina, stone-faced, stared back without speaking.

Deena pressed on. "His prints were on the gun."

Still nothing.

"So, what makes you think your brother was murdered?"

"I have three reasons." She held up her hand to tick off each point. "For one, his wife wanted him dead. Number two, she was cheating on him. And number three, he wasn't depressed like the police said, and he wouldn't kill himself." She stuck out her chin as though she'd just had a drop-the-mike, slam dunk moment.

Deena looked back at the notepad and scribbled down the list. Everything Edwina had stated was circumstantial. "Are you saying you think your sister-in-law, Allison, killed your brother?"

"That's exactly what I think." She paused, then added, "Poor Andrew. He didn't deserve that. He was nothing but good to that woman and to me." A few tears slid down her cheek.

Deena passed her a tissue. "What would Allison's motive have been to kill her husband, in your opinion?"

"Money, of course! That's all she ever wanted." More tears came now.

This sounded like a typical case of grief overtaking reason. Some people just couldn't accept the fact that their loved one was gone, especially by his or her own hand. Maybe she should suggest a grief counselor or support group.

The desk phone rang and Deena could see it was from Paulette. She lifted the receiver and said, "Not now, I'm busy," and hung up. She handed Edwina more tissues as the phone rang again. "Paulette, I'm with a client—"

"I know, Ms. Deena, and I wouldn't call you if it wasn't important, but it is."

Deena waited for more. When Paulette didn't speak, she gritted her teeth and barked, "What?"

"Oh," Paulette said, "Mr. Davis wants to see you."

"Did you tell him I was with a client?"

"Yes, ma'am, but he said it had to be *right now*."

"Okay," Deena said, hanging up. The woman was still blotting tears. "I'm sorry, Ms. Granger, but I have an urgent matter. I'll be right back."

Deena left the office and closed the door behind her. She couldn't imagine what was so important that Ian had to interrupt a client's interview.

He was standing next to his desk when she walked into his office. His tie was loose and his jacket was thrown over the credenza. He motioned for her to take a seat. She recognized the grave expression on his face as the one he used when delivering bad news.

Suddenly, she felt a grip in her chest. "What is it? Is it Gary? Did he have an accident?"

"No, no," Ian said, holding up his hands. "It's nothing like that. Everyone is fine."

She let out her breath and released her white-knuckle grip on the arms of the chair. "Then what?"

"It's about...your job here."

Uh-oh. This didn't sound good.

Ian stared down at his hands. "I'm afraid I can no longer have you working for me."

Deena's jaw dropped. "But you promised you wouldn't replace me while I was out covering for Sandra."

"I know, and I haven't replaced you, not yet anyway."

He sat down on the corner of his desk. "It's the funding from the state. They've changed some of the requirements and are offering incentives for public defenders to hire employees who are in the system."

"What system?"

"The legal system. Like people on parole or on probation. It's part of the reintegration program."

Deena nodded slowly, afraid if she spoke she might cry.

"I know how excited you were to be back, I just wasn't aware you'd be here today. I was working up my nerve to call you when I found out you were here with a client." His eyes showed genuine concern. "You know how many pro bono cases I handle. If I had the money, I would absolutely have you here, you know that."

The phone rang and Ian picked it up. "Give me just a minute, Paulette." He held the receiver against his chest and looked mournfully at Deena. "Are you going to be all right?"

She wiped away a lone tear traveling down her cheek. "Sure. I understand."

Ian put the phone back to his ear. "What is it, Paulette?" After a brief pause he said, "Okay, I'll tell her."

He stood up and walked back around his desk and sat down. "It seems the woman you were meeting with wasn't keen on waiting."

"You mean she left? Did she leave a phone number?"

"Nope. She told Paulette to tell you she'd be calling you in the next few days. Paulette gave her your cell phone number."

"Oh my." There were so many questions Deena had wanted to ask her, like, why did she think Allison was cheating on Drew and why hadn't she talked directly to the police?

Ian drew in a deep breath. "Under the circumstances, I suppose you need to tell me what she said." He reached for a pad of paper.

Deena nodded. "Fine. But hold on to your hat. This is going to be a tricky one."

Chapter 4

DEENA HAD WORKED BRIEFLY for the *Northeast Texas Tribune* before getting fired for failing to follow the editor's directive to stay away from a murder investigation after she had found the body. She had remained friends with fellow reporter Dan Carson, who had recently taken over as news editor. Sitting across from him in his office, she worried about how much more stressed he looked than the last time she'd seen him.

When he hung up the phone, he unbuttoned the top of his shirt and loosened his tie.

Like most women, Deena wondered why men still bothered wearing neckties since most men (Gary excluded) seemed to despise them. If women could give up pantyhose, men should be able to lose the ties.

"Sorry to keep you waiting," he said. "How have you been?"

"Peachy," she said. "What about you? You look like you could use a vacation."

"Not a chance. We're short-handed as is. Although, I was thinking of taking a long weekend with Lydia over spring break."

"I was wondering if you two were still together. Is she feeding you well?" Deena had played matchmaker for the couple.

Dan patted his slightly bulging gut. "Too well. Now, what can I do for you?"

Deena pulled a piece of paper from her handbag. "Have you ever heard of a woman named Edwina Granger?"

"Granger? Sure, she's part of that Granger's Grapes clan. Why?"

"She came by to see me today."

Dan sat upright in his chair. "Really? I didn't realize she was back in town. One of my reporters tried to get ahold of her for the Andrew Granger suicide story, but he didn't have any luck. Which is to say, he probably Googled her, found no phone number, and gave up." He rubbed his forehead.

"Real in-depth reporting there," Deena said and laughed.

"You have no idea." He loosened the second button on his shirt. "So, what did she want with you? Is she Davis's client?"

"Oddly, no. She said she'd heard about my reputation as a...um, murder-solver, and she wanted me to look into the death of her brother."

"Not surprising. From what I assume, the family fortune is all going to Granger's wife. She probably wants in on the action."

Deena frowned. "So, you don't think there's anything there? I mean, you doubt his wife staged the suicide?"

"The wife? It's possible, of course. You know that. Have you talked to the police?"

"No. I came straight here from work. I mean, my former work. I got 'let go' today." She emphasized the phrase with air quotes.

Dan revealed a slight grin. "Sorry to hear that."

"You don't look sorry."

"That's because I have an idea. Come back to work for the paper."

Deena crossed her arms. "Um, I was fired by Lloyd Pryor, in case you've forgotten."

"Come on, I need a crime reporter and you need a job."

"I don't know," she said. "I've gotten pretty used to working part-time. Now that the baby is here—"

"What?" Dan's eyes narrowed. "You had a *baby*?"

"No, silly. Sandra and Ian's baby. Gary and I are the godparents."

"And Ian still canned you? Some friend." Dan balled up a piece of paper and threw it across the room, missing the trashcan by a foot.

"It wasn't like that. It was a funding issue. Anyway, I want a flexible schedule to be able to help Sandra out at the thrift store if she needs me."

"How about this." He leaned forward. "The greenhorns out there in the news division can handle the minor stuff, and we'll only call you in for the big stories."

"Big, like what?"

"Like investigating the possible murder and cover-up of one of the area's most notable residents." He steepled his fingers as though masterminding a heist.

It was a tempting offer. Deena was planning to nose around into the case anyway. The prospect of getting paid to do it was certainly enticing. Then she remembered why she had gone to work with Ian in the first place. He was all about helping people who couldn't help themselves. Dan was cynical and saw the world through dark-colored glasses.

"I don't know," she said. "I don't like the idea of looking for the bad in every situation."

Dan shook his head. "It's not about finding the bad, kiddo. It's about finding the truth. Isn't that why you majored in journalism? Isn't that what you taught your high school students?"

"Yes," she said slowly, "but most of the time the truth is pretty ugly."

"But justice," he said through a sly grin, "Lady Justice is a beautiful thing."

Dan had always been able to sweet-talk her. Still. "Can I talk to Gary and get back to you?"

Dan's face fell. "Your husband doesn't particularly like me."

"That's not true. He's just protective of me. I'm sure you're the same way with Lydia."

"Okay, but you better make it quick. You can't come in here and drop a juicy lead like this and not expect me to follow up on it."

"I know," Deena said and stood to leave.

"By the way, why did Edwina Granger go to you instead of the police?"

Deena bit her bottom lip as she thought about it. "I don't know. She disappeared before I had a chance to ask her."

"Interesting. We need to track her down. Could be she knows a lot more about her brother's death than even the police do."

Deena wasn't sure she liked Dan using the word "we" to talk about the investigation. But maybe a part of her still wanted to be a journalist. Maybe that's why she came to Dan instead of going to the police.

Here we go again.

Chapter 5

GARY CAME HOME FROM work that day with a "special surprise." He'd already given Deena a pink opal pendant for their anniversary, and she couldn't imagine what her loving husband might have had that would be any better. Maybe this was what he meant when he said he would "make it up to her" when they had to go to Drew Granger's funeral on their anniversary.

She held out her palms and closed her eyes as he dropped something in her hands. It didn't feel like jewelry. Her fingers touched it and she guessed it must be a gift card. A free massage, perhaps? She opened her eyes and read aloud, "'A one-month free couples membership to Never Too Fit.'" It was the new gym that had just opened in Maycroft. "Wow. I didn't expect *this*." She tried to hide her disappointment.

"I know! Isn't it great?" Gary's face didn't reveal anything other than excitement.

How could they have been married all these years and he still not know how she would feel about this sort of "gift"? Apparently, moments like this kept the marriage interesting.

"I guess we'll have to check it out sometime," she said, giving him back the card.

"Not sometime, now. I made us an appointment with the trainer for six thirty. I'll make us a quick sandwich while you go change."

Deena hadn't even told him about her job yet. She was waiting to break it to him over dinner. Maybe if she dropped the f-bomb now, he would feel bad for her and reschedule their appointment. She gave it a shot. "I got *fired* today."

Gary was halfway to the kitchen when he stopped in his tracks. "Fired? By Ian?"

Deena tilted her head and tried to work up a few tears. "Well, technically, I was let go. But either way, I lost my job."

Gary walked back and wrapped his arms around her. "I'm sorry. I know you liked your job. But just think, this will give you more time at the gym."

She pushed him away and took a step back. "Are you kidding? Is that supposed to make me feel better?"

Like a cartoon comic strip, she could practically see the gears churning over his head. His shoulders slumped, apparently realizing he'd been caught in a husband-trap. "I'm sorry," he said, "but you know I didn't like you working with criminals at Ian's law firm. The work you did had a dangerous side. I guess I was being selfish."

The hurt in his eyes stirred up Deena's guilt. After all, Gary had always been generally supportive every time she'd fly off in a new direction. Chances were, he wasn't going to be thrilled with her working as a crime reporter, even if it was only part-time. It would be better to wait until the mood was right to spring it on him. Maybe exhaustion from working out at the gym would weaken his resistance.

"Okay," she said. "I'll get changed."

Gary grinned and headed to the kitchen.

Deena had given it a lot of thought all afternoon, and the more she mulled it over, the more certain she was that she wanted to give it another shot at the newspaper. Edwina Granger had said Deena was known for her talent in investigating murders, and that had boosted her ego.

But now, standing in front of her dresser trying to decide what to wear to the gym deflated her big head. She hadn't worn workout clothes since Sandra had dragged her to that yoga class. That was way before Sandra had even gotten pregnant. Deena pulled a pair of black stretchy pants out of the drawer and held them up. They looked like some little girl's ballet tights.

She slid in one leg and then the other, trying not to tip over as she worked the waist of the pants up over her thighs and hips. She could barely breathe, but they were on. She chose a long, loose t-shirt and then attempted to put on her sneakers without cutting off the circulation to her torso.

She looked in the mirror at her flushed face. "This is certainly going to be fun," she muttered.

NEVER TOO FIT COULD have been called *Never Too Fresh*. The stench of sweat and sports gel hung in the air like a heavy fog as they signed papers at the front desk. The gray floor, gray walls, and black equipment made the place look even more depressing than Deena had imagined. The few people working out wore headphones and looked about as happy to be there as patients in a dentist's waiting room.

Deena felt her muscles begin to cramp just standing there.

A buff bodybuilder in a too-tight t-shirt walked up and grabbed Gary's hand. "Hi. I'm Marcus. You must be the Sharpes. Come on in and we can get you warmed up."

Deena trailed Gary as they were led through the torture chamber. She eyed the steel contraptions suspiciously, wondering which one was going to send her to the chiropractor. Deena had managed to stay fairly fit while she was teaching, but once she quit, things started to change. Her late fifties were a struggle, and now that she'd turned the big six-o, she felt like a bear preparing for hibernation.

Marcus stood next to the foreboding treadmills. "The key to a good warm-up is getting a light sweat. It's your body's way of saying it's ready for the big stuff."

More like ready to head home. She wanted to fake a coughing spell and leave, but the excited look on Gary's face stopped her.

Marcus looked her up and down. "Am I right that it's been a while since you two have worked out?"

"That depends," Deena said. "When was Ronald Reagan in office?"

"That's funny, Mrs. Sharpe," Marcus snorted and gave her a playful jab on the arm.

That's gonna leave a mark. She rubbed her arm and said, "Call me Deena, then call me an ambulance."

Gary grinned. "I play golf and swim laps a few mornings a week at the Y, but you better start with the basics. Deena's more of a newbie."

That was putting it mildly. It would have been easier to just wait a few minutes. She was bound to get a hot flash.

"How about you try five minutes on the treadmill. That should do it." Marcus proceeded to explain the controls. "After a couple of minutes, kick it up a notch and try jogging. When you feel your legs start to burn a little, you can slow down." He flipped on the switch to start the machines.

Deena held on to the rails and began walking slowly. She gave Marcus a thumbs-up sign.

"I'll be back to check on you in five," he said and headed over to a brunette on a stationary bike.

This wasn't so bad. But about a minute in, she felt her legs begin to ache and her feet felt numb. Maybe she had tied her sneakers too tight. She pressed on.

Gary had increased his walking pace and turned to look at her. She smiled, which was a mistake. He reached over and turned up the speed on her treadmill.

She felt like the roadrunner with legs whirring around at lightning speed as she held on for dear life. Although she was still just walking, her legs protested as though the friction from her thighs rubbing together had inadvertently caught her pants on fire. Sweat dripped from her armpits and more beaded on her forehead. She dared not let go to wipe her face for fear of flying off the back of the death trap.

Gary adjusted his speed again into a steady jog. Her pride kept her from screaming. A minute later when he looked over at her, she shot him a look of pure terror. He switched off his machine to check on her.

"Are you okay?" he asked.

She shook her head. "I'm done."

Gary turned off the treadmill as Marcus walked up, his face showing his concern.

"Are you all right? You better sit down over here." He led her to a bench while Gary fanned her with a towel.

Marcus grabbed a bottle of water and poured some out on another towel and draped it across Deena's neck. "Wow," he said. "I've never seen anyone turn that shade of red so fast before. I thought you might be having a heart attack." He chuckled, then added, "Thought we might have to break out the defibber."

Good one, Deena thought. *Let's make fun of the old, out-of-shape woman on her first day at the gym.*

Once her breathing had slowed and some of the redness had faded from her face, Gary suggested they call it a day and head home. Not wanting him to be disappointed, she insisted that she let Marcus work with him while she rested.

Gary jumped at the offer.

Deena walked back to the front desk to check out the gym's amenities. Maybe they had a whirlpool or sauna she could take advantage of the next time Gary dragged her up there.

This was more like it. The other side of the gym had steam rooms, Jacuzzis, massage rooms, and a smoothie bar with a lounge area. She grabbed her wallet and cell phone from Gary's gym bag, ordered a banana smoothie, and settled back in an overstuffed lounger. She was happy as a clam. Only thing that could make this better would be to remove her shoes, but she was afraid they might not go back on.

One message beckoned her from her phone. It was from Dan Carson at the newspaper. She read: "You need to make your mind up quick. Just got a hot tip on the Granger story. Are you in or out?"

Without a second thought, she typed her reply: "IN."

A smile crossed her face. She didn't need a workout to get her juices flowing. Dan had her hooked. Now all she had to do was tell Gary.

Less than a minute later, her phone beeped. The message from Dan made the hair on her arms stand up. It read: "Allison Granger is pregnant."

Chapter 6

MAYCROFT HAD ONE LOCALLY owned and operated bank. A few of the big chains had small satellite offices, but most people entrusted their money to the First Bank of Maycroft. That's where Deena headed the next morning a few minutes after Gary kissed her goodbye and left for work.

Deena had told him about the new job offer at the newspaper but left out one little bitty detail. She didn't tell him she would be covering major crimes in the area. Since the Grangers were Gary's clients, she didn't want him to feel like there would be a conflict of interest. Besides, the whole thing might turn out to be nothing. Edwina Granger could just be another jealous relative trying to get her hands on Allison's money.

Dan had dropped another bombshell, although she shouldn't have been surprised. The editor-in-chief, Lloyd Pryor, had said she could work at the newspaper on a trial basis. He would make a final decision about hiring her back after she finished with the Granger case.

After talking to Dan, Deena wasn't sure how his source's tip about Allison expecting a baby played into the accusation that she might have killed her husband, but you never knew. Did Drew know he was about to become a first-time father when he shot himself? That's not a normal reaction. Or maybe Allison hadn't yet told him.

Dan and Deena had cooked up a plan to say she was writing a feature article on Drew, and that Deena wanted to set up an interview with Allison. She would feel the widow out to see how receptive she'd be to granting a sit-down with Deena.

The bank had a homey feel. No armed guard stood by the door and there was a waiting area with hot coffee and cold water for customers. It wasn't unusual to run into an acquaintance in the lobby and sit for a spell to visit.

Deena spotted Allison behind one of the old-fashioned teller windows and got in line. The white-haired woman in front of her held a paper sack in one hand and her pocketbook in another. She obviously had a bagful of coins to cash in. The bank had one of those new-fangled coin counters, but the tellers usually just counted everything by hand because of the gosh-awful noise the machine made.

On the dark paneled wall behind the tellers hung an old portrait of the late Alexander G. Maycroft, the bank's first president and the great-grandson of the town's founder. His beady eyes stared at Deena as if warning her to mind her p's and q's. Of course, it could have just been her own conscience. She didn't really like to lie even if it was a means to an end. In this instance, it could lead to justice for Drew Granger if he had indeed been murdered.

Just as she was contemplating the ethics of her position as an investigative reporter, the woman in front of her went to another teller.

A minute later, Allison signaled for Deena to step up to the window. "How can I help you today?" she asked without looking up.

"Hi. I'm Deena Sharpe."

Allison's cheeks flushed. "Oh, I'm sorry, Mrs. Sharpe. I didn't see you. I guess I'm in a bit of a fog today." She forced a smile.

Wearing a navy pantsuit with a flowy white blouse, Allison appeared softer and more vulnerable today. Her blond hair was pulled back in a ponytail and her makeup was less severe.

"Please call me Deena. I'm sure it's been hard for you to get back to work."

"Well, yes. This is my second day back. So, how can I help you? Got a check to cash? Need to make a withdrawal? Here to rob the place?"

Bank humor. Deena tilted her head and used a sympathetic tone. "Actually, I'm here to talk to you."

Allison squinted and leaned back on her stool. "Me? Why?"

"You see, I'm writing an article on your late husband for the *Tribune*, and—"

"What kind of story? Don't you think they've smeared his name in the paper enough already?" She crossed her arms tightly as though to give herself a comforting hug.

Deena's mouth went dry. She hadn't expected this reaction. "It's—it's a human-interest piece on him as a businessman and community member. It's like a tribute."

"Not interested," Allison said. "Now if you have no banking needs, I'd appreciate if you would just move on."

Why was Allison being so defensive? Deena tried to stall. "Actually, I need to withdraw a hundred dollars from my account."

Rolling her eyes, Allison slid the withdrawal slip toward Deena.

She filled it out and slid it back, saying, "In one-dollar bills, please."

Allison pursed her lips and opened the cash drawer. She picked up the stack of ones, put a rubber cap over her thumb, and began counting. "One, two, three..."

"Allison, I didn't mean to upset you," Deena lowered her voice to a whisper. "Don't you want to honor your husband for the good things he did?"

Ignoring her, Allison continued counting. "...sixteen, seventeen..."

"I can come to your house and we can talk about it. You don't want people just to think of him as that man who killed himself, do you?"

"...thirty-one, thirty-two..."

Deena let out a sigh. "If not for yourself, do it for your child."

Allison froze as she stared at Deena. "How do you know about the baby?"

Shrugging her shoulders, Deena said, "It's a small town."

Looking back at the stack of bills, Allison picked them all up and stacked them together, carefully aligning the edges. She began counting again. "One, two..."

Obviously, Deena had the girl rattled. She might as well ask. "Did Drew know about the baby?"

Tears began to well in Allison's eyes. Then, without warning, she choked out what some may have thought was a confession. "It's all my fault! It's my fault he's dead!" Throwing the bills on the ground, she ran into a back office.

The other teller moved quickly over to Deena. "Oh dear! What happened?"

Deena threw up her hands. "I don't know. Paper cut, I guess."

Chapter 7

MOST OF THE TIME, CASEWORKER Nina Davenport looked forward to weekly staff meetings to discuss the kids' progress at the Boys Respite Ranch. Today, however, she knew it would be a challenge.

"Why the glum face?" Mary Boyd asked as she took her seat next to Nina at the conference table.

To be clear, the table wasn't one of those big mahogany jobs surrounded by high-back swivel chairs with armrests. It was actually two card tables pushed together to seat five metal folding chairs and one with worn vinyl padding reserved for Dr. Kyle Patton, the head psychologist at the youth facility.

"Lucas," Nina said and sighed.

Mary nodded, indicating she knew full well that Dr. Patton and Nina had vastly different opinions on the boy's progress. "Just don't get emotional," she cautioned Nina. "Dr. Patton responds better to facts than to sob stories."

Nina fingered the stack of folders on the table in front of her. "I know, but there's some things you just can't measure with numbers."

A man with a graying ponytail and a diamond stud in one earlobe opened the door and entered as though he were the guest of honor at a party. With his threadbare jeans and Nirvana t-shirt, Dr. Patton looked more suited for a biker bar than a boys ranch in the middle of the Nevada desert. "Good morning, my friends. Sorry to keep you waiting."

The four counselors smiled, not letting on to the fact that they had long ago started showing up to the eight-thirty meetings at five till nine, knowing the good doctor had never once made it on time. It is not unusual for those in power to have narcissistic tendencies, and making others wait on him was one way that particular characteristic manifested itself in Dr. Patton.

After settling into his thrift store reject of a throne, he opened the meeting with his usual quip. "Now who's first up on the chopping block?"

Nina stopped herself from an eye roll. You'd think he'd come up with new jokes after eight years. But Mary was right. Nina was indeed in a particularly foul mood today. Might as well get it over with.

"I'll go first," Nina announced. "Let's start with Lucas Carr. I feel he's made good progress, and I'd like to see him transition back home."

There. She'd said it.

Dr. Patton drew circles on his notepad. Without looking up he said, "Details. He's barely been here five months. What makes you think he's ready?"

She opened the folder to the extensive notes she had made and scanned the list. Nothing she had written seemed that convincing. If only Dr. Patton knew Lucas like she did, he would understand. Sometimes a kid just needed a chance to prove himself.

Closing the folder, she clenched her hands under the table and rested them in her lap. "He's homesick. That's why he's started acting out again. But that doesn't mean he hasn't been meeting his treatment goals. For instance, yesterday he opened up in group about his relationship with his stepfather. He knows he contributed to the problems in the family and wants to try again to work things out."

Dr. Patton appeared unmoved. "How can you be so sure he wasn't just telling you what you wanted to hear, and when he doesn't get his way, his behavioral issues will resurface?"

"There's no guarantees in this business, we all know that." Nina glanced at her colleagues. "But taking responsibility for his actions is a huge step."

"Yes, it is," Patton said and nodded. "And a breakthrough like that is a good start. But we also know that maintaining what he's learned will be difficult when he returns to the home environment and all its stressors."

Nina could feel her shoulders tense as she chose her words carefully. "I agree, but we also know that once a child feels ready to return and isn't allowed to be given a chance to prove himself, he can shut down or give up. I'm afraid that's what will happen to Lucas."

Just then, the door opened and Belinda, one of the house parents, entered with a strained look on her face. She stepped tentatively toward the group. "Sorry to interrupt, but I need to speak to Nina for just a minute. It's about one of the boys."

Dr. Patton waved her closer. "Spit it out, Belinda. If it's important enough to interrupt my meeting, let's hear it."

She wrung her hands and looked at Nina apologetically. "It's Lucas. The new boy, Porter, accused him of stealing his sneakers and they got into a fight."

Nina's mouth fell open. "But Lucas wouldn't steal."

The woman replied softly, "I found the shoes under Lucas's bed."

Nina glanced at Dr. Patton. His expression was even more smug than usual.

Although she refused to be defeated, it was times like this she wondered if she should have just stayed in Maycroft.

Chapter 8

WHEN DEENA FINALLY spilled the beans about her new job and the new case, she was shocked that Gary was so supportive. It was even his idea to go with her to the Granger's Grapes winery the next morning to talk to Lonnie.

As they wound their way through the piney woods, Deena wondered what had come over her once so predictable husband. "Gary, are things okay at work?"

His eyes darted from the road to her and back. "Of course. Why wouldn't they be?"

"It's just that you've been acting a little...off lately. First, those few mornings you overslept, then the gym membership, and now you're taking off work to spend the day helping me. Well, half a day, that is. It's just not like you." She studied his reaction closely, watching for signs of anger or resentment. Gary had never been too complex, and she could generally read his thoughts without much trouble.

He snorted a dismissive laugh. "It's a beautiful day, not too cold for this time of year. Can't a guy take a day off occasionally to be with his beautiful wife?"

"Not when he's Gary Sharpe. I can't remember the last time you missed a day of work."

"Don't be silly. I missed work on Monday, on our anniversary."

Deena crossed her arms. "That was for Drew's funeral. You went back to the office afterward."

He fixed his gaze on the road as he gave it more thought. "What about last fall? We spent the day together, remember?"

"We were picking up one of your clients from the airport."

"Oh, that's right." He furrowed his brow. "Well, regardless, everything is fine. You can't blame a guy for wanting to take a drive out to the country every once in a while, especially when there's wine involved." He grinned and gave her a pat on the knee. "Tell me, how are we going to play things with Lonnie Fisher? Good cop, bad cop? He'd never believe me as the bad cop, so you better do that."

Deena sat in silence. In the past, Gary always groaned and moaned about her investigative exploits, causing her to keep some of the more harrowing details to herself. Now, here he was not only supporting her sleuthing but wanting to be an active participant.

"We just want to find out what was going on those last days before Drew died. Maybe he can confirm that Drew was depressed and his death was just a tragic suicide. Case closed."

Gary frowned. "Case closed? Just like that?"

Deena wasn't sure what to say. Obviously, she would try to track down more information, but did she really want Gary to know everything she was doing? Although he'd always been her emotional compass, he'd never been her sidekick. "We'll see," she answered, not committing to anything.

* * *

GARY LED THE WAY INTO the office building where he had occasionally met with Drew and Lonnie to discuss financial matters. They were greeted by a frumpy secretary named Vera Clausen who seemed to be holding on for dear life to her nineties color-block windbreaker, big hair, and saucer-like gold clip-on earrings. Deena hadn't seen anyone dress like that since she'd gone with her mother-in-law, Sylvia, to Friday night bingo.

"I'm so sorry, Mr. Sharpe, but Mr. Fisher asked me to tell you he was running a few minutes late. You can wait in his office if you'd like."

"That would be fine, Vera," Gary said.

Vera started down the hall to the left of her desk with Deena and Gary trailing behind. Suddenly she stopped and turned around.

Deena and Gary almost tripped as they barely stopped from tumbling over each other like a line of dominoes.

"Oh, dear me," she said as she walked around the pair. "I still haven't gotten used to Mr. Granger not being here, bless his heart." She wrung her hands. "Mr. Fisher's office is this way." She led them past her desk to the other hallway.

Deena saw an opportunity to snoop. "Do you mind if I just freshen up first? It was a long drive."

"The ladies' room is right over there." Vera continued around the corner with Gary.

Deena waited until they had disappeared down the hall before heading to Drew's office. The nameplate on the door was a sad reminder of the boss who wouldn't be coming back to work. Making sure she hadn't been followed, she closed the door behind her.

Either Drew had been a neat freak or someone had straightened up his office. It was tidy as a pen. She walked around the desk and found two framed photos. One was of Drew and Allison. The other was of Drew and Lonnie. She scanned the bookcase, not really knowing what she was looking for. There were a few trophies and plaques all dedicated to the winery and vineyard. Nothing really seemed to give her a glimpse into Drew's personal life.

A leather-bound calendar sat on the credenza, flirting with her to open it. She did. Nearly all of the date squares were filled in. She flipped to the current month just as she heard the sound of heels clicking out in the hallway. They stopped outside Drew's door. Who was it? She was certain Vera had been wearing an old pair of Keds rather than heels. She set down the calendar and held her breath. What would she say if someone came into the room? She tried to think of an excuse, but her mind went blank. The doorknob turned, and then she heard muffled voices. The clicking sound began again and faded away.

That was too close. She let out her breath slowly before hurrying out the door and back around the corner.

As she hurried past Vera's desk, Deena grinned. "Oops. Wrong way." She walked down the other hall into the opened office door and found Gary and Lonnie talking amiably.

"You made it," Gary said. "You remember Lonnie."

Deena reached out to shake Lonnie's hand. His grip was firm as he squeezed her hand with increasing pressure until she nearly winced in pain. The gold ring on his hand dug into her fingers. It was all she could do not to look down and check for blood.

"Nice to see you again," Lonnie said when he finally let go. His phone buzzed and he answered.

Gary motioned for Deena to take a seat. He leaned in and whispered, "Everything okay? You look flushed."

"I'm fine," she said through gritted teeth, shaking out her aching fingers.

Lonnie and Gary could almost be brothers except for the fact that Gary was a foot taller and twenty years older. They both had salt-and-pepper hair and were dressed in polo shirts with crisply creased khakis. Lonnie wore a pair of canvas deck shoes just like a pair that sat in Gary's closet. No wonder the two got along so well.

As he listened to the voice on the other end, Lonnie's eyes drifted toward Deena. Was it Vera ratting on Deena?

After hanging up the phone, Lonnie narrowed his eyes. "Why don't we go over to the tasting room for our conversation. I have a couple of new bottles you might want to try out."

Gary's face brightened. "Sounds good."

Lonnie waited for Deena and Gary to exit the office, then pulled the door firmly behind him.

Deena had a feeling Lonnie found out she'd been snooping around. She needed to get on his good side.

Lonnie stopped outside the building housing the tasting room and turned to Deena. "Mrs. Sharpe, have you ever had the opportunity to stomp grapes?"

"Call me Deena, and no, I haven't."

"Ah, just as I thought." He motioned toward a large barrel. "You must give it a try. There's nothing like the feel of what the French call *pigéage*."

Deena pictured the several days of hair growth on her legs and her unpainted toenails. "I'm sure it's delightful, but I think I'll pass."

"Please, it would warm this vintner's heart." He clasped his hands and gave her a pleading look.

"C'mon, Deena," Gary said. "When will you ever get another chance like this?"

Deena forced a smile. *Traitor.* "I guess I might as well."

"Excellent!" Lonnie led her to a bench where she removed her shoes and rolled up her slacks. He held her hand while she made her way up the ladder on the side of the barrel, all the while hoping he didn't stare at her legs or feet.

She threw her leg over into the dark purple mush. It reminded her of when her brother, Russell, made her go with him to a haunted house where they walked across "eyeballs." It wasn't until some years later she found out they were just rubber balls.

She gripped the sides of the barrel and took a few obligatory steps. "Fun," she said, hoping to sound convincing. She turned to get out.

"Not yet," Lonnie said. "Give it a good stomp. Really get your toes into the fruit. Remember, wine is the blood of the gods, and you are making a sacrifice."

Sighing, she marched in place until she stepped on something sharp. "Ouch!" She reached down and looked at her purple foot. A trickle of blood appeared on her big toe.

Lonnie covered his mouth with his hand. "I forgot to warn you about the stems." She couldn't tell if he was apologetic or amused.

Gary helped her out and went inside with Lonnie while she hosed off. The sticky violet goo clung to her legs, looking like bits of guts and blood.

She found Gary and Lonnie inside the tasting room chatting about the latest harvest while Lonnie poured Gary a flight of four different wines. Deena wandered around admiring the Italian décor and various products for sale. She had never seen wine-flavored dog biscuits before and debated getting some for Hurley.

"And for you?" Lonnie asked as he set the wineglasses on a small table in front of Gary.

"I'll just have some water," she said, wanting to keep a clear head. "One of us has to drive."

Lonnie motioned for the hostess to bring the water and sat down, crossing his legs casually.

"You really should try this Tempranillo," Gary said, giving her a signal with his eyes.

Oops. She got the message. It was probably rude not to at least try the wine at a winery. She needed to butter Lonnie up if she hoped to get any real dirt about Drew and Allison. "I'll just have some of yours," she said, and chugged the remainder of the glass. "Yum. That was delicious. Really...sweet."

Gary grimaced as he turned to Lonnie. "Actually, this is a dry wine. I have to apologize. Deena doesn't know much about wine, other than red and white."

Lonnie smirked. "I understand. We can't all have an intelligent palate."

Deena bristled and stuck out her chin. "Chocolate."

Lonnie cocked his head at her. "I beg your pardon?"

"I'm a connoisseur when it comes to chocolate," she said defiantly.

"Is that so." Lonnie handed her one of Gary's wines. "And what chocolate would you pair with this Zinfandel?"

She sniffed the glass as she'd often seen Gary do, then took a sip. She smacked her lips together a few times before answering. "Swiss." She stated it with an air of authority.

"I see. Are you sure you mean chocolate and not cheese?" He grinned smugly, then he and Gary chuckled.

Ugh. What nerve. Who was to say what chocolate goes with what wine? It's not like she had said Hershey's. "Let's get to the interview, shall we?" She reached in her handbag for her spiral and pen. "Tell me what you think people should know about Andrew Granger now that he's gone."

Lonnie gave the usual answers, including Drew's successes in business and personal attributes like being a hard worker and having a good sense of humor.

Deena wrote a little and doodled a lot. This, of course, wasn't the information she really cared about. She nodded at the appropriate times and asked a few follow-up questions.

Whether it was the bottle of wine or just letting him talk, Lonnie seemed to relax and even take a liking to Deena. She put away her notebook and then asked to try a small glass of Lonnie's favorite wine.

He popped out of his seat with a big smile on his face and headed to the counter to get it.

Once he was out of earshot, Deena whispered to Gary, "What do you think?"

"About the wine? I wasn't too keen on the Viognier but the Albariño was excellent."

"No," she said. "I mean about Lonnie. Do you think he'll give me any of the real dirt on Drew?"

"As long as you keep kissing up to him. Be sure to rave about the—"

"Here you go," Lonnie said, and set the glass in front of her. "This is a 2010 Bourbon Barrel Cabernet. I think you'll see it hits all the right notes."

"Thanks." She took a sip and tried not to gag. The red liquid burned on its way down her throat and then performed a somersault in her stomach. "Wow. I've never tasted anything quite like that."

"Let me have a sip," Gary said. He nodded in appreciation. "You can really pick up the vanilla notes. I was expecting the Cab to be more spicy, but it was actually quite smooth."

"Lonnie," Deena said, "you were obviously a close friend of Drew's. Were you surprised when he...killed himself?"

He darted his eyes as though a pain shot through his body and he was trying to hide it. "Yes and no. You see, I knew he was having trouble at home. He wasn't happy with Allison. I think he felt trapped. In fact, he told me they hadn't been intimate in quite a while."

"Really?" Deena wondered if Lonnie knew that Allison was expecting. That would contradict the lack of intimacy. "How well do you know Allison?"

"We get along fine," he said as he leaned back in his chair. "She was never much involved in the business. I'd see her occasionally in social settings. She was quite possessive of Drew."

"Possessive, how?"

"She didn't like him working late or hanging out with the boys." He looked down at his hands. "I don't think she ever particularly liked me." Then he drifted into silence.

Deena stared at the ring on Lonnie's hand and remembered the aggressive handshake. She took a fake sip of the wine and gave Gary a nod to signal that he should finish it. While Gary drank, Deena waited to see if Lonnie would continue. Finally, she asked, "Has Allison talked to you about the business? Surely she plans to keep you on to run things."

Lonnie brushed away a piece of lint from his slacks. "I don't know. Like I said, she and I never really got along that well. In fact, anytime I came to the house, she'd conveniently have someplace to go, like the salon or shopping or like that last night when she was at her book club."

"Last night? What do you mean?"

Lonnie took in a deep breath. "The night Drew shot himself, she was at her book club."

"And where were you?"

The question seemed to startle him. "Why do you ask?"

"You said that Allison would leave the house when you came over and then you said she was at her book club. Were you at Drew's house that evening?"

"No. He invited me to the house to play cards, but I was busy."

"Busy doing what?"

"Mrs. Sharpe, I'm not sure I like your tone." He stared at her with furrowed brows.

Gary broke the tension. "We've taken up too much of your time, Lonnie. We should be getting on our way." He stood up and reached out to shake hands with their host. "We really appreciate your time, right, honey?"

"Of course." She knew she was in hot water with Gary. He always called her "hon." When he was ticked off, he'd call her "honey" or even "Deena Jo."

Gary put his hand on her back and pushed her gently toward the door. "Here's the keys. Why don't you wait for me in the car. I can't leave without buying a few of these wines."

Deena took the keys and headed outside. Was Lonnie Fisher hiding something? Obviously, there was bad blood between him and Allison. Maybe he was worried about losing his job.

She stared in the visor mirror waiting for Gary. She saw him exit the tasting room. Lonnie patted his back. Apparently, they had played good cop, bad cop after all, and Gary seemed to still be in Lonnie's good graces.

As soon as they got back on the main road, Gary let her know how he felt. "Deena, the man lost his best friend, and you practically accused him of conspiring to have him killed."

"Conspiring? What on earth do you mean?"

Gary shook his head. "Don't tell me you weren't implying that Lonnie and Allison had something going on on the side."

"Um, I wasn't. I swear. But now that you mention it..." Deena's head spun with the possibility. Edwina Granger had said Allison was cheating on Drew. Could Lonnie be covering up the affair by telling people he and Allison didn't get along?

She calculated her next move. Gary would drop her at home and head back to work. Then it would be time to pay a visit to her favorite police detective. Maybe she could worm some information out of him.

Chapter 9

LINUS GUTTMAN HAD GROWN a beard since Deena had last seen him. It served to strengthen his weak jawline and soften his dark eyes. He had put on a few pounds, which helped fill out his too-slender frame.

Deena wondered if maybe he'd finally found a lady friend. He'd had a hard time adjusting to small-town, Southern life since moving here from Philadelphia.

"What do you want?" he asked in his usual Yankee manner.

Deena just smiled at him across his desk. "Nice to see you, too, Detective Guttman."

"Don't tell me you found another dead body. Did you kill somebody this time or are you just here to harass me?"

Deena snickered. "While all those possibilities are tempting, I'm here on business."

"I see. You still working with that attorney, Ian Davis?"

Ian was a defense attorney who worked with legal aid. Naturally, he and Guttman were adversaries.

"No. As a matter of fact, I'm back at the *Tribune*."

Guttman scratched his new beard. "Didn't you get fired from there?"

She flinched at the f-word. "That's all water under the bridge. But actually, I'm working on a trial basis and I need your help."

The detective had good reason to eye her suspiciously. Deena had been either a thorn in his side or a confidant on several cases. He probably wasn't sure which she would be this time. "Like I said, what do you want?"

"I'm writing a feature on Andrew Granger. A tribute. I wanted to see if you could tell me anything about his death."

Guttman cocked his head. "That's not usually the sort of thing you put in a feature story. Besides, the paper already ran stories about his suicide. Time to move on."

Deena had anticipated Guttman's resistance. In the past she'd been able to wriggle loose bits of information if she was persistent enough. After thirty-something years as a high school teacher and then through her various stints as an investigator, she'd gotten pretty good at getting information she wanted. Adults were often more transparent than teenagers, but Detective Guttman would be a hard nut to crack. She was prepared to be patient.

She tilted her head coyly. "I know, but there were some details missing from those stories that I thought you might fill in."

"Like what?"

"Like who found the body and who the responding officer was. Also, did he leave a suicide note? Did he own the gun he shot himself with?" Deena reached in her purse for a notepad and pen.

"All that info is going into a tribute to the man?" Guttman leaned back in his chair and crossed his arms. "Give me a break. What are you really up to?"

She hesitated before letting out a sigh. "Look, you're right. I got a tip that maybe Andrew Granger's death wasn't a suicide, but instead was a murder."

Guttman remained expressionless. "A tip. Seriously, Mrs. Sharpe, you know better than to listen to every crackpot conspiracy theory that comes along. Tell me about this tip."

She shook her head. "I can't. It was confidential."

"You expect answers from me but won't tell me who you've been talking to?"

"I can't reveal my sources, you know that." She hugged the notebook to her chest.

"Sources." The detective sat upright and reached for a folder on his desk. "Just so you know, my guys thoroughly investigated that scene. Asked all the right questions. The last thing I need is the press stirring up trouble where there isn't any."

"But—"

"No *buts*, Mrs. Sharpe. That's it. I've got work to do. Thanks for stopping by."

She stood to leave. "Okay, but you know I'm not going to stop digging."

"I'm sure you will."

She opened the office door and turned back. "You look good, by the way. I like the beard."

He nodded. "So does Officer Linndorf."

Puzzled by the comment, Deena closed the door behind her. Officer Linndorf? Larry Linndorf? What was that about? She made her way out to the parking lot and then it hit her. Guttman had thrown her a bone. Officer Linndorf must have been the responding officer at the Granger house when Drew was found dead. That's why he was talking to Allison at the reception. She was sure of it. But why didn't Guttman just come out and say so?

It seemed like there was another mystery behind the mystery.

* * *

DEENA MAY HAVE BEEN starting over as a cub reporter, but it didn't mean she was without her own sources. She called one she knew she could trust and asked to be notified when Linndorf was spotted.

As a former journalism teacher, Deena had taught her students how to write the perfect news lead, how to organize facts in an inverted pyramid, and how to properly attribute quotes. But never having had on-the-job experience as a real reporter had left her unprepared for what crime reporters had to do to sluice out the real story. Luckily, her experience as an investigator with Ian Davis's law firm had helped her get her hands dirty and had shown her what it took to get to the truth. That, along with her natural curiosity—or what Gary would refer to as nosiness—had prepared her for this assignment, and she was determined to do whatever necessary to get to the real story behind Drew's death, even if it turned out to be suicide.

But if he had killed himself, something had led him to that point, and Deena wanted to know what it was. She sat at the desk in her home office and started organizing her notes. It wasn't long before her cell phone rang. She recognized the number and answered. "Yes?"

"The eagle has landed," mumbled the voice on the other end of the line.

Deena checked the name on the phone again and put it back up to her ear. "What are you talking about?"

"Linndorf. He's at the doughnut shop."

"Oh, thanks," she said and chuckled. "I didn't realize you were using code. I'll drop by to see you later." Deena hung up.

She looked down by her feet. Hurley, her black terrier, looked up expectantly. "Sorry, boy. You have to stay here. I'm on an assignment."

Deena grabbed her notepad and headed out the door to make the short drive to downtown Maycroft.

Her secret source was her best friend, Sandra Davis, her ex-boss's wife. It was the kind of entanglement common to small-town life. The donut shop that the local cops frequented sat across the parking lot from the thrift shop Sandra managed. All Sandra had to do was keep her eye out for a police car and call Deena when she spotted Linndorf. Sandra already knew about the case Deena was investigating from her husband, Ian. Sandra had insisted Deena stop by after talking to Linndorf to give her an update.

Deena had gladly agreed. She'd get a chance to hold her goddaughter and shop for vintage treasures at the same time.

Linndorf was seated in a booth near the back reading the *Tribune*. He looked up as she approached, but then returned to studying the sports page.

Larry Linndorf wasn't what you would typically call handsome. His eyebrows needed a serious trim and his teeth were crooked. But he had boyish dimples and bright blue eyes that many women would find attractive. She had encountered him a number of times in the past when working on various cases. She had always thought of him as courteous and semi-competent.

Deena cleared her throat with all the subtlety of a lion's roar. When he peeked back over his newspaper, she started in. "Officer Linndorf, I was wondering if I could have a few minutes of your time to talk about Andrew Granger."

That got his attention. "You're Mrs. Sharpe, right?"

"Call me Deena." She stuck out her hand to shake and hoped he wouldn't mash it as hard as Lonnie Fisher had. "I just spoke to Detective Guttman and wanted to ask you a few questions for the article I'm writing for the paper about Andrew Granger." Everything she said was true, although she left out the detail that the detective hadn't exactly given her the okay to interview him.

"You talked to Guttman?"

She nodded.

Linndorf motioned for her to sit. "Want some coffee?"

"No, I'm fine," she said. "I understand you were the first officer on the scene when Mr. Granger was found dead. Is that right?"

He folded his newspaper, then took a drink from the oversized mug. "Well, yes and no. I was the first officer to respond to the call, but I didn't know Mr. Granger was dead until after I got there. The caller had said she was worried about someone in the house."

Deena pulled out her notepad. "I see. And who was the caller? Allison Granger?"

He raised an eyebrow. "No. It was the neighbor. Said she heard a loud noise and went to check on it. She called into the station."

"What happened when you got there?"

"I went inside and found Andrew Granger with a bullet in his head and a gun by his side. Not a pretty sight."

"Was anyone else there? Did he leave a note?"

"He was alone. No note."

"And how did you know it was a suicide? Did you check for gunshot residue on his hand?"

"GSR? No, of course not. You see, it doesn't take a genius to figure out when a man has shot himself at close range. I'd rather not explain all the gory details, but it was obvious."

"But aren't those the details you need in order to rule out a murder? How are you so sure it wasn't just staged to look like a suicide?"

Linndorf narrowed his eyes. "Are you sure you talked to Guttman?"

"Yes," Deena answered. "You can call him if you'd like."

Apparently, her demeanor portrayed enough confidence that he waved it off. "Hmm. Anything else?"

"Just one more question. The gun. Who was it registered to?"

"Andrew Granger, that's who." He checked his watch. "I've got to get back out there." He stood up and tossed a few bills on the table. "If you think of any other questions, call Guttman. He knows this case as well as anyone."

"I'll be sure to do that." She sat for a moment thinking about Linndorf's last comment. If Guttman was so familiar with the case, why did he put her onto Officer Linndorf? Was there something about Linndorf that Guttman wanted her to find out for herself? She had a feeling there was more to the investigation than Linndorf had told her.

Sensing something was missing, she left the coffee shop more determined than ever to figure out what it was.

Chapter 10

WHEN THE STAFF MEETING was finally over, Nina Davenport headed to the dormitory to check on Lucas. The door was open, so she knocked and went on in. Lucas was sitting on the edge of his bed while Belinda paced the floor.

"What's going on here?" Nina looked to Belinda for an answer.

Lucas saw her and ran over and hugged her around the waist. At eleven years old, he was smaller than most of the other boys his age. According to his chart, he was initially a failure-to-thrive baby until his mother separated from his real father and moved in with her aunt. That was before his mother remarried and Lucas began acting out.

Belinda took a seat at the small table. "Lucas refuses to take responsibility for stealing Porter's shoes. I've just been explaining how the consequences will be less severe if he just admits what he did."

Nina peeled Lucas off her waist and knelt down in front of him. "Lucas, did you take Porter's shoes?"

"No, Ms. D." His eyes were moist, but he wasn't crying. "I swear I didn't."

Nina brushed back his sandy-brown hair. "Okay, then. I believe you."

A relieved expression crept across his face.

Belinda let out a groan. "Ms. Davenport, could I speak to you in private in the hallway?"

Nina stared into Lucas's dark hazel eyes. The specks of gray-blue had returned. "I'll be right back."

Belinda pulled the door closed behind them. "Nina, I know how much you care for the boy, but the facts are clear. Lucas took those shoes and hid them under his bed. Another boy said he heard Lucas talking about them."

"Talking about them and stealing them are two different things."

Belinda shook her head. "How else did they get there?"

"I don't know, but I plan to find out. Let me talk to him."

"And what about the fighting?"

"Yeah, that's a problem." Nina wrung her hands as she looked back at the closed door. Playing referee between staff and the residents was one of the hardest parts of the job. "I'll try to get to the bottom of the situation. Where are the shoes?"

"I gave them back to Porter. They are both restricted to their rooms for now. Please don't let Lucas go outside. It will send a bad message to the other kids."

Nina agreed. "I'll come find you after I've talked to him."

She went back inside Lucas's room, being sure to leave the door propped open. He was lying on his bed, his hands behind his head. She sat at the small round table and waited for him to speak first.

At last, he did. "I want to go home."

"I know you do. So do most of the boys here. But you know we have to be sure you're ready. Can you tell me what happened with Porter?"

Lucas threw his legs off the bed and sat up. "I was at the barn brushing down Shiloh. These younger kids come up with Porter. He's acting all tough like he's lord of the flies or something."

Nina couldn't help but grin. She loved the fact that Lucas was an avid reader and would often use stories to make analogies.

"So, I ask what's up and he says he wants his shoes back. I tell him I don't have his shoes. He says, 'Oh yeah? Brandon saw you take them.' But Brandon wasn't even there. I told him he was crazy and started back brushing Shiloh."

"Do you think that was the best choice of words? Could you have said something besides calling him crazy?"

"I suppose I could have said, 'Kind sir, perhaps you are mistaken.'" He said it with a corny British accent. "'Perhaps we should call on Sherlock Holmes to track them down.'" He twirled an invisible handlebar mustache.

Nina had to laugh. "I have a feeling that would have gotten you flattened."

"Probably."

"So, what happened?"

"He called me a liar and pushed me. He knocked me into Shiloh and she reared her head. That made me mad. I didn't care that he pushed me, but he shouldn't have scared the horse. So, I pushed him back." He looked down at his feet. "You don't have to say anything. I know I could have made a better choice."

Nina waited. Sometimes being a counselor was so hard. What she wanted to say was that she'd have probably done the same thing. It was natural to resort to your fight or flight instinct, but these kids just had to learn to avoid confrontation whenever possible. "So, what could you have done instead?"

"I could have asked him why he thought I took them and said we should find an adult to work it out."

Smiling, Nina nodded. "Very good. So why didn't you?"

"I don't know." He lay back down on the bed, nearly hitting his head on the rail of the top bunk.

Nina pulled her chair closer. "I think you do."

Lucas turned his head away and made a huffing sound. "I didn't want those other kids to think I was a coward."

"And why do you care what they think? Aren't you supposed to be a role model here for the younger boys?"

"Yes."

"And was getting in a fight setting a good example for them?"

"No."

"Then why—"

Lucas jumped off the bed and stood squarely in front of Nina. "Because it felt just like being at home. I get in trouble when I lie and I get in trouble when I tell the truth. What does it even matter if I'm always getting blamed for everything that goes wrong?"

Nina's heart ached and she wished she could throw her arms around the boy and tell him everything would be okay. But the truth was that it wouldn't. Sometimes in life we are falsely accused of things. Sometimes we are bullied, even as adults. The important thing is to learn to deal with these situations calmly and rationally. But many adults couldn't seem to learn that, much less an eleven-year-old boy.

"Sit down, Lucas." She pointed to a chair. "Remember, while you've been here, your parents have been going to counseling back home. I've gotten good reports that they're working hard to make things better for when you go back."

"Do you know when that will be?"

Nina hated that question, whether she heard it from Lucas or any other boy. Since she was just a counselor, only Dr. Patton could sign off on the release of a child. This latest incident would likely cause an even longer delay. Since Lucas had been mandated by the court to be there, even his parents couldn't bring him home without the psychologist's consent.

"We'll see," Nina said and placed her hands flat on the table. "But for now, we've got a mystery to solve. We have to figure out how those shoes got under your bed."

"Somebody else put them there. They were trying to *frame* me."

"Who do you think it was?"

"Well, if we deduct it right—"

"Deduce," Nina corrected him.

"Deduce it right, it was probably Brandon since he told Porter he saw me take them."

"That sounds plausible."

Lucas squinted and tilted his head. "What?"

"*Plausible*. It means that it is a good guess."

"Plausible," Lucas repeated. "That's a cool word."

"Look, you stay here while I go see what I can find out about the situation."

"Thanks, Ms. D."

Nina stood up just as Belinda came into the room pulling Porter behind her. She avoided eye contact with Nina. "Lucas, Porter has something to say to you."

The boy had been crying and stared down at his feet. "Sorry I lied."

"And what else," Belinda prodded.

"I know you didn't take my shoes. I lied and said Brandon snitched on you."

Nina looked at Lucas.

"That's okay," he said. "I shouldn't have pushed you back."

Porter looked up, obviously surprised by the apology. "Sorry I hit you."

Belinda nodded. "Okay, that's enough for now, boys. We'll talk more about this later."

As Belinda and the boy were halfway out the door, Lucas called out to him, "Porter. Why'd you do it?"

The other boy stopped and looked back. "I wanted the other guys to think I was tough. I didn't want them to call me a sissy."

Lucas nodded. "Next time make a better choice."

Nina and Belinda exchanged looks. Moments like this were few and far between in their line of work, but these were the times that made it all worthwhile.

Waiting until they were alone, Nina stood by the door and looked back at Lucas. "I'm proud of you."

He grabbed his neck and made a gagging face. "Whatever. I'm still on restriction for now, right?"

"Right. There's still the matter of fighting."

He picked up a book off the wooden shelf next to the bed and lay back down. "I figured that was plausible."

Chapter 11

AS THE GARAGE DOOR opened, Deena was surprised to see Gary's car there. She hadn't expected him home for at least another hour. Naturally, she worried something was wrong. She hurried inside to check on him. She found him sitting in his recliner watching a basketball game with the sound muted. His tie hung unknotted around his neck and his top button was open.

"What's wrong?" She glanced around and found Hurley curled up in his usual spot. "Is it your mother? My brother? Did you get fired?"

"No, none of those. It's me."

"Are you sick? Are you dying? Are you leaving me? Because if you're leaving me, I just might kill you."

Gary put the footrest down on his chair and patted his leg for her to come sit in his lap.

She could feel her heart beating out of her chest. "No. Tell me before I drop dead."

"Really, hon. Everything's fine."

"Then what is it?" She sat on the edge of the coffee table, her purse and keys still in her hands.

"I've just been thinking that it might be time for a change."

"Like what? You're not thinking of moving to Tulsa to be closer to your mother, are you?"

"No. I was thinking of starting my own business."

Relief swept through her. She set down her things and moved over to the sofa. "Is this about you and Scott wanting to set up your own finance firm? I've told you before that I think you should do it. Together, you two have plenty of clients, and—"

"It's not that. I was thinking of starting my own winery."

Deena wasn't sure she had heard correctly. "Did you say winery? As in dirt and grapes and such?"

"Yes. You see, driving out to Granger's Grapes got me thinking. Do I really want to spend my last good years trapped in an office?"

"Yes. You do. You definitely do."

Gary began rolling up the sleeves of his dress shirt, something he rarely did. "Think of it. You and me out in our very own field planting vines. You would be in one of those flowy dresses like they wear in *Mamma Mia!* I'd have on a straw hat and a plaid shirt. We'd be tilling the soil and creating a lasting legacy."

Deena leaned back. "Tilling the soil? You don't even like mowing the grass and cleaning the pool. Do you really see yourself with your hands in the dirt?"

"I saw Lonnie's hands. They didn't look too bad."

"Of course not. He works in the office. They pay other people to work in the field."

"Maybe now, but I'm sure he and Drew spent their share of time in the fields getting the vineyard to the point it is now."

Deena walked over to Gary and sat in his lap, wrapping her arms around his neck. "Listen, I understand if you're tired of your job. It happened to me, too, a few years back. That's why I quit teaching. But maybe you just need a vacation. You've been begging me to go to Italy. Maybe it's time we take that trip."

"It's more than that. It's having to put on a suit and tie every day and going to an office."

"But you love your suits. You love your ties. Besides, you said you wanted to work until you were sixty-seven to maximize your retirement. That's only six and a half more years. That will fly by and then we can move to a retirement community and you can play golf every day."

Gary let out a heavy sigh. "Six and a half years. That's two thousand three hundred and seventy-three days, not including leap days."

Deena stood up and took his hand. "See there. You're a math genius. You're not a farmer. Let's fix some dinner and have a glass of that new wine."

Gary stood up and trudged toward the kitchen. "I could have been a farmer if I had wanted to."

"Of course you could have. Just like the Grangers."

Deena's thoughts turned back to Allison Granger. Maybe she was tired of her life, too. Could she have killed her husband to have money to start over? Did he have a big life insurance policy? How much exactly was Granger's Grapes Vineyard actually worth? Gary would know, but now wasn't the right time to ask him.

If she wasn't careful, he might start thinking he should buy their vineyard himself.

Chapter 12

HUNCHED DOWN IN HER SUV, Deena waited until she saw Allison Granger pull out of her driveway and head off to work. *Bankers' hours*, she thought. *Must be nice to leave for work at a quarter till nine.*

When Deena had taught high school, she was one of those teachers who arrived early and stayed late. She attributed it to meeting deadlines for the school's newspaper and yearbook. Years later she finally admitted to herself that it was to avoid going home to an empty house and waiting for Gary. They hadn't been able to have children, and all the high school kids she taught had never really been able to fill that void.

But what she needed now was to find the Grangers' nosy neighbor. Perhaps it was a stay-at-home mom or retired curmudgeon who considered himself captain of the neighborhood watch.

After seeing Allison turn onto the next street, Deena drove right up to the house and parked at the curb. She practically sprinted to the door and rang the doorbell, fully expecting it to go unanswered. She waited a minute and then pounded her fist on the door and called out Allison's name.

She looked at the house to the right of the Granger residence. The two houses were separated by both driveways. If someone were inside that house, they would be unlikely to hear her. She glanced to the left. The two-story red-brick colonial with the first-floor shades raised was her best guess at the house whose occupant she hoped to attract. She thought she saw movement inside.

It was time to pull out all the stops. She held her cell phone to her ear as though making a call and began moving up to each window and cupping her free hand as though trying to peer inside. Of course, all the curtains were drawn and she couldn't see a thing. Still, she knew she would raise concern from a curious neighbor.

Sure enough, an older woman wearing what her mother used to call a "house dress" came from around the side hedge. "You just missed her," the woman said. "She's gone off to work. Can I help you with something?"

Deena flashed a grateful smile. "Oh darn. I guess I'll have to come back next week...unless...no, never mind." She started toward her car.

"Unless what, dear? Maybe I can help."

Deena stopped and turned back to the woman. "Well, I guess it wouldn't hurt to ask. You see, the insurance company just needs a few more details about what happened on the day of her husband's demise before they can issue her check. You wouldn't happen to know anyone who was around at the time, would you?"

The woman's eyes widened. "As a matter of fact, I do. I was the one who called the police to come over here and check on the noise."

"Really? What luck! Would you mind if I ask you a couple of questions? I'm sure Mrs. Granger would be grateful for you helping out."

Taking Deena by the elbow, the woman led her toward the house. "Why, I'd be pleased to help out. Let's go in and have some coffee and I'll tell you all about it. I'm Barbara Potts, by the way."

"Nice to meet you, Barbara." Deena was careful not to give the woman her own name. One lie at a time. It wasn't exactly her motto, but she hoped the end would justify the means

When they went inside, Deena counted three cats lounging in a pile by the window and a caged green bird. Poor Barbara. She must be a kind, lonely widow. But then she heard a gruff voice call out from the kitchen.

"Barb! What are you up to now?"

"Shut up, you old coot! I've got company!" Her tone was anything but kind. She turned back to Deena and smiled sweetly. "Cream and sugar?"

"Fine," Deena said, hoping she wouldn't raise the ire of the four-foot monster in front of her.

When Barbara returned with the coffee, Deena had visions of *Arsenic and Old Lace.* She blew in the cup and set it down without taking a drink. She pulled out her notepad and turned to a clean page. "Can you tell me what happened that day?"

"Well now, I was sitting in the living room watching *Law and Order.* It was a good one, too. That man...what's his name? You know, the one who does those commercials?"

Deena shrugged and shook her head.

"Well, anyway, I heard a loud noise. At first I thought it was a car backfiring. But then I remembered that cars don't do that much anymore, so I ran to the window. It was dark, you know, but I saw a car speeding the other direction down the street."

"Did you get a good look at the car?"

The gravelly voice from the other room yelled, "She hasn't seen anything clearly since before her hair turned purple!"

"Shut your trap, Harry!" Barbara roared. She looked back at Deena and calmly said, "No, I could just see the tail lights. Anyway, I thought I would go check on poor Allison to see if she was okay."

"Why were you concerned about Allison?"

"Well, I'm not one to gossip, but I had seen the police over there more than a few times. I wanted to make sure that husband of hers hadn't done something to her."

Deena got a heavy feeling in her chest. "Do you think something bad was happening to her? Like maybe Drew was hurting her?"

Barbara's brow wrinkled even deeper than it was already as she leaned in, lowering her voice to a whisper. "I had my suspicions, not that I ever saw anything or heard them out of sorts, but one day I tried to ask her about it."

Deena waited. The dramatic pause was killing her.

Jerking back upright, Barbara's expression turned sour. "She told me to mind my own business and quit being such a busybody. Can you believe that? If I hadn't been such a caring neighbor, she'd have come home from her party and found her husband dead on their marriage bed!"

Harry yelled, "You old gossiping hen!"

Rolling her eyes, Barbara said, "Excuse my husband for his *rude manners*!" The last two words were screamed like something out of *The Exorcist*.

Deena scooted a little further away on the sofa. "So, you were saying you wanted to check on Allison."

"Yes. I went over and rang the bell and nobody answered. I knew somebody was home because I could see lights on. That's when I tiptoed over to the window and took a peek inside."

The elusive Harry called out again. "She's a regular Peeping Tom, that one is."

Just then the large bird piped up. "A peeping tom. A peeping tom."

"Quiet, Jack! Good Lord, a person could go crazy around here."

Deena's eyes widened at the commotion. *Lady, you passed crazy on Thursday.*

"Anyway, that's when I called the police."

"Wait," Deena said, "why did you call the police?"

"Oh, I thought I told you. I could just make out Mr. Granger's legs on the bed. But when I tapped on the window, he didn't seem to hear me. That's when I ran to get Harry. He told me to call the cops, so I did. I was standing right out there by the front door when that nice-looking officer showed up."

"Do you mean Officer Linndorf?"

"Yes, that's the one. I'd like to make some 'law and order' with him, if you know what I mean." She grinned and her top dentures slid back and forth.

Deena almost threw up in her mouth at the thought of Barbara and Larry Linndorf. "What did you see when you all went in the house?"

"Oh, he didn't let me go in with him. He told us to wait outside."

Deena gave that some thought. "Did you go around to the bedroom and 'peek' while he was inside?" She used air quotes to emphasize the seediness of the action.

"I wanted to, but Harry wouldn't let me."

Jack the bird chimed in again. "A peeping tom. A peeping tom."

Barbara pulled off a slipper and hurled it toward the birdcage, missing by a country mile.

Deena shook her head. "How long was it before Officer Linndorf came out of the house?"

"He didn't come out, I mean, not before the ambulance and other police cars got there."

"How long was that?"

"Well, it seemed like forever because I was standing there in my housecoat and slippers. The wind cut through me like ice. I'd been telling Harry I needed to get me one of those robes they have on TV that doubles as an electric blanket, but he said I'd probably burn the whole house down." She tossed a look in the direction of the kitchen and yelled, "With you in it!"

"So...ten minutes?"

"That sounds about right."

"And where was Allison?"

"I think she was out. Seems like the next day she said she'd been at a party."

"Party? Are you sure?"

Barbara took a gulp of coffee, then coughed into her hand. "Yes. Like a Tupperware party."

Did they still have those? "Tupperware? Are you sure?" Deena looked at Barbara, who seemed to be thinking.

"No, maybe it wasn't that." She looked around the room as if the answer could be hidden in the corner behind the old bookshelf. "She mentioned a book." Snapping her bony fingers, she said, "That's right! A book party!"

Book party, book club. Tomato, to-*mah*-to. Close enough. "Do you know anyone else who was at that book party?"

"Heavens, no. Allison never invited me, so I never asked." Barbara shivered and grabbed her cup. "Drink up, dear, you don't want your coffee getting cold."

Without thinking, Deena picked up the cup. When it was almost to her lips, she looked down and saw a clump of cat fur floating on top. She sneezed and sent coffee flying everywhere. She had managed to stave off the reaction until then, but now her eyes began to water and her throat itched. "I'm so sorry! It's just that I'm allergic...*choo!*...to cats." She stood up and hurried to the door. "Thank you for the information. It will really help with my article."

Barbara looked puzzled. "Article?"

"I mean...*choo!*...report. Bye now." She closed the door behind her and hurried to the car, sucking in breaths of cool clean air as best she could. She grabbed a wad of tissues and blew her nose. When she looked in the mirror, her eyes were already red and puffy. As she drove off, she saw Barbara and a man who she assumed was Harry standing on the front porch waving good-bye. Harry had his arm draped over Barbara's shoulder. She was, of course, wearing only one slipper.

The sight of the old couple made Deena grimace, and she made a mental note to be nicer to Gary about his desire to make a change.

Speaking of Gary, it was time to talk to him about Drew's business as well as his supposed *devotion* to his loving wife. It's not like Drew Granger deserved to die, but if he had been abusing Allison, that might be a motive for murder.

Chapter 13

AS SHE WALKED OVER to the staff meeting, Nina dreaded facing Dr. Patton. She had managed to avoid him since last week's meeting when they discussed Lucas. She had a feeling she'd get a big fat "I told you so" at this week's meeting.

Mary Boyd caught up with her. "I think I know the reason for the glum face this week. Lucas, right?"

Nina nodded. "There's no telling how long he will be stuck here now. Doc will probably stretch it out longer just to show me who's boss."

"Dr. Patton can be reasonable sometimes. You just have to catch him in the right mood." Mary shuffled her folders to the other hand as she reached for the doorknob. "But you're right. Most of the time he's—" She caught her breath and whispered, "—here. He's already here."

Dr. Patton steepled his fingers while resting his elbows on the table. "Glad you ladies finally decided to join us. By my watch it's nearly nine o'clock."

Nina and Mary hurried to take their seats just as their last colleague came in.

"Whoa," he said as he spied the doctor. "Sorry I'm late."

Dr. Patton scowled. "Seems everyone was running late today. No matter. I'm in a good mood."

The four counselors just stared and waited.

"Isn't anyone going to ask me why?"

Almost in unison, they all asked.

"Because, the foundation renewed our grant for another three years, which means we won't have to cut staff after all."

"I didn't realize you were looking at cuts," Nina said. "Guess we dodged a bullet."

"A bullet indeed," Dr. Patton said. "Now, who's first up on the chopping block?" He held his hand up. "No, wait. I'm going first."

The counselors exchanged glances. It was unusual for someone as OCD as Dr. Patton to change up his routine.

"Nina, I want to show you something." He pulled a folded-up piece of notebook paper out of his satchel and handed it across the table.

Her heart began to beat a little faster. Surely she wasn't getting fired. He just said he didn't have to make cuts. She opened the note and began to read. It was addressed to Dr. Patton. She skimmed through quickly. One sentence was highlighted in yellow. It read: *Ms. Davenport has made me a better person and I want to show my family that I can be just as good a person as she is.* Nina's eyes began to water as she read the rest and then saw the signature at the bottom. It was from Lucas Carr.

Nina sniffled once and looked up at Dr. Patton. "I didn't tell him to do this, if that's what you're thinking."

"I'm not thinking that at all. I'm thinking you've done a remarkable job with this boy. I've read all your case notes and have planned. We're going to transition Lucas to go home."

The other three counselors clapped their hands, a tradition whenever they moved a child to the transition program.

Nina couldn't help herself. She jumped up, ran over to Dr. Patton, and threw her arms around his neck. "Thank you, thank you, thank you," she gushed.

The doctor stiffened but allowed the embrace. "Good job, Ms. Davenport. Now, who's next?"

The rest of the meeting was a blur. Nina felt as though she were sitting a foot above her chair. Nothing could make her day any better.

After the meeting, Nina headed over to the main office to start Lucas's paperwork right away. As she walked past the area where the staff received their mail, she noticed a large manila envelope in her cubby. Since she rarely got mail, it piqued her interest. Maybe she'd won a prize or something. She ripped it open and began reading. She felt the color drain from her face and her knees shook.

Mary walked by and noticed the look on her face. "What is it now? I thought you'd be elated."

Nina looked up from the letter. "It's my brother," she murmured. "He's dead."

Chapter 14

LUCKILY, THERE WERE only a few cars parked in front of the drugstore when Deena pulled up. She needed eye drops and an antihistamine to deal with the allergy attack from Barbara Potts's cats. She put on her sunglasses and went inside.

She walked past the makeup counter and caught a look of herself in the mirror. She looked like a spy in a Bond film. All that was missing was the floppy straw hat. She found the aisle she needed and noticed a man looking at the cold relief products. He looked vaguely familiar, which was not uncommon in a town the size of Maycroft.

The man glanced her way, holding a bottle of pills. "Hey. Cold. How about you?"

"Allergies," she responded and tilted down her sunglasses.

"Geez. Looks like you've got it bad."

"I'm not exactly the Elephant Man, but yeah. It's bad." She picked up a package of super-strength antihistamines, then looked back at the man. "Do I know you from somewhere?" She hoped he didn't think she was trying to hit on him, not that her current appearance would have been too appealing.

"Um, not that I know of."

Then it hit her. This was the same man from the funeral who told Allison he wanted to make sure Drew was "good and dead."

"Hope you feel better," he said and started to walk off.

"Wait. Weren't you at Drew Granger's funeral?"

Jerking his head back, he stared at Deena. "Er...um...yes. Why do you ask?"

"I just noticed that you spoke to Allison as though you weren't too fond of her husband."

The man's ruddy face turned a funny shade of red. "Maybe I was out of line saying something at his funeral. But if you knew why, you wouldn't fault me for it."

"Oh," Deena said, "I'm not doubting your motives. Drew Granger was no saint after all. Am I right?"

"You're right." He shook his head.

Deena was hoping to get more juice from this lemon. "So, what did he do to *you*?" She emphasized the "you" to imply she had a beef with the man, too, as though they were comrades in arms. Yes, she was tricky like that.

"Put me out of business, that's all."

"That's all? Why, that's terrible. What happened?"

He pulled a handkerchief out of his pocket and blew his nose. "Ah, you don't want to hear."

"Sure I do," she replied earnestly. "How'd it happen?"

"It's been probably fifteen years now since he and that no-good brother-in-law of his ravaged my property and stole some of my best, oldest grapevines. Claimed it must have been some people from out west, but I knew good and well it was them."

"I see, so you have a vineyard, too?"

"Did. After that, everything went downhill. The Grangers undercut my prices at every turn. Pretty soon, no one would touch my crops. They actually accused me of stealing from the Grangers. Can you believe it?"

Shaking her head, Deena gave him her most sympathetic expression. "That's terrible."

"I'm Owen Walsh, by the way." He started to reach out his hand to shake, then looked at the cold medicine box and pulled it back.

"Nice to meet you." She quickly added, "Did you get the police involved? Did you sue him?"

"Tried to, but no one believed the Grangers with their 'grapes from God' would do such a thing. I eventually sold my land to Drew and his sister for a fraction of its worth."

"His sister? I didn't think he had a relationship with his sister. Does he have more than one?"

"Not that I know of. Yeah, he and Edwina took over the place when the old man got sick. That's before their father disowned Edwina."

Deena could hardly believe what she was hearing. Sounded like Edwina could definitely be trying to get her hands on the Granger fortune. But she wasn't the only one who had a beef.

Deena went for the jugular. "Man. If someone had done that to me, I'd have wanted to kill the guy. Am I right?"

That's when Owen Walsh clammed up. Whether she was touching on a nerve or whether he thought she was a monster, she wasn't sure. But as quick as she could say "ah-choo," he had bid her good day and was gone.

As she made her way to the checkout counter, Deena thought about Drew. Maybe he did kill himself, but it's not like there weren't other people waiting in line to do it for him.

* * *

GARY HAD JUST GOTTEN there when Deena arrived back home to her cozy house in the suburbs. Actually, Maycroft was too small to have official suburbs, but that's how townspeople referred to the Butterfly Gardens neighborhood development.

Their little slice of the town had all the trappings of stereotypical suburbia, including nosy neighbors, ultra-competitive Little League dads, overprotective helicopter moms, cookie-cutter houses, and minivans or SUVs in almost every driveway. Deena liked it there.

Even though she felt safe, she sometimes felt out of place. Because she and Gary had no children, they often got hit up to buy the neighborhood kids' fundraising merchandise. By her calculation, she could make it through twenty more years of holidays without having to purchase another roll of wrapping paper. The deep freezer in their garage had more tubs of cookie dough than Ben and Jerry's. And as it turned out, those expired coupon books made great kindling in the winter during the two weeks it was actually cold enough for a fire in northeast Texas.

Deena waved at a few of her fellow suburbanites who stood at the edge of the lawns checking their mailboxes. Since Gary was already home, he would have beat her to it.

She went inside to find her husband sitting at the kitchen table with a big grin on his face. She prayed silently that he hadn't turned in his two weeks' notice at work. "Hey there. What's going on?"

Gary grimaced when she took off her sunglasses. "What's wrong with your face? You're all red and puffy."

"Cats." She knew that was enough of an explanation for now.

He nodded and the smile returned to his face. "You're never going to believe this." There was a twinkle in his eye. "I have a surprise for you. You might want to sit down."

Oh dear. What was it now? A personal trainer? A coupon for ballroom dance lessons? A time share at Disney World? She slapped on a nervous smile and waited.

He held up a large manila envelope. "Guess who's been named a beneficiary in Andrew Granger's will?"

"You? Are you kidding?" Deena's eyes nearly popped out of her head as she grabbed the envelope.

"I can save you from reading through a lot of legalese. It basically talks about probate and creditors and potential exclusions, but that I am named as a beneficiary. Also, Allison has requested an old-fashioned reading of the will and it is being held at the attorney's office on Monday."

"This coming Monday?"

"That's correct."

Deena fanned herself with the envelope. "You know what this means, don't you?"

"That I have to take off another morning of work?"

"Yes, but also it means you and I will get to be there when the will is read. You know how it is on TV. That's where they almost always figure out the murderer."

Gary seemed to have trouble searching for the right words. "We, I mean, me. I mean, only I was named in the will, not both of us."

"Pish-posh," she said, waving her hand. "Minor detail. We're Gary and Deena. No one is going to think twice if you bring your wife along."

He looked at her like she was the cat who ate the canary.

She grinned back at him. "Don't worry. I'll be on my best behavior."

Gary let out a deep sigh and nodded. "I'm going to hold you to it."

She kissed his cheek and pulled out her notes. "Are you ready to get caught up on the case?"

"Sure. Fire away."

She told him about Officer Linndorf being the first responder and how he hadn't really even considered murder as an option and had failed to do the usual tests. She also told him how the neighbor—the cat lady—said the cops were sometimes at the Grangers' house, which worried her about Allison's safety.

Gary rubbed his chin. "I would be sick to find out Drew had been abusing Allison. He didn't seem like the type. However, we know that abusers come in all shapes and sizes, and you can never tell what goes on behind closed doors. Did you ask Linndorf if they had any police reports on it?"

"No. I talked to the neighbor *after* I spoke with the officer. I plan to ask Detective Guttman about that very thing tomorrow. I'll get to the bottom of it."

As Gary walked into the bedroom to change out of his suit, Deena went to her office to email her editor Dan with an update. The case was still a puzzle with more pieces being added every day. Although there was still no hard evidence of a murder, there seemed to be a lot of finger pointing in this case. Most of those fingers pointed to Allison. Not only had she literally said she may have caused her husband's death, but her sister-in-law had also suspected her. Lonnie Fisher had also implied the Grangers had a troubled marriage.

But now there was Owen Walsh. He, too, seemed to have a strong motive. But why now after all this time? And would he really be bold enough to show up at his victim's funeral?

Gary was right. You never knew what went on behind closed doors. That was true for what went on in a killer's mind as well.

Deena needed answers fast. The reading of the will was in two days. She wanted to narrow down the suspects so she could unmask the killer in dramatic fashion. She knew Gary would forgive her for making a scene.

But only if she were right.

Chapter 15

THE PRESS CAN BE A powerful force when it comes to seeking justice. All Deena had to do was threaten Detective Guttman with running a story about the underwhelming police work performed on the Granger case to get him to agree to meet with her at the diner on the outskirts of town. It was the same one where she used to meet with Dan to talk about cases and articles they were writing.

She fantasized that when she walked in, Clara, the waitress, would greet her with open arms and ask if she wanted "the usual."

In reality, the haggard waitress thrust a menu at her and said, "Find a spot."

All the booths were taken by the local senior breakfast crowd and weary truckers needing a hearty meal and a break from the miles they'd traveled down the long Texas highways.

Deena found a table near the back. She debated taking off her sunglasses. Her nose was still red but the puffiness around her eyes had subsided a little. She put the glasses in her handbag and waited for Clara to bring coffee.

To her disappointment, the waitress obviously didn't remember her. Clara poured the coffee, splashing some onto the table, and groaned that she'd be back to take her order. Deena didn't even have a chance to tell her she was waiting on someone to join her.

Deena pulled out her notes and studied the questions she planned to ask Guttman. Most of them centered around Allison as well as the investigation itself. She was locked and loaded, ready for bear.

When Guttman came in, Deena waved to get his attention.

Clara was all over him, smiling and escorting him to the table. "Aren't you just the tallest, yummiest drink of water I've seen in here in a while," she crooned. "Where have you been all my life, handsome?"

The fact that Clara was thirty years older than Linus Guttman didn't seem to bother him at all. Was that a blush she detected under that dark beard? Indeed, it was.

Clara poured the coffee and pushed the cream and sugar closer to his mug.

Geez. It wasn't like he couldn't reach the extra six inches to get it himself. Deena felt nauseous just watching the over-the-top display of flattery.

Clara seemed disappointed when Guttman said he'd already eaten and would only be having coffee. She didn't even bother to ask Deena for her order.

After Clara left the table, Deena grinned at Guttman. "Looks like someone has a new girlfriend?"

He stopped midair as he was pouring artificial sweetener into his cup. "How did you know?" He looked around as though a state secret had just been uttered in front of the enemy combatants.

"I was kidding," she said. "Clara...the waitress..."

"Oh, that," he said with an air of relief. "I get that all the time."

Now Deena was surprised, not by the fact that he didn't catch her humor—Guttman had always been pretty strait-laced—but by the fact that he was used to flattery and apparently had a new friend.

Deena probed. "Who's the lucky lady? Someone on the force? The new owner of the bakery on Elm? Clara's daughter?"

"Not a chance. Don't even ask." He blew in his cup and took a sip.

Deena patted her chest. "You know that it's not against the law to be dating someone. You're allowed to be happy."

"Let's stick to the reason you called me here, Mrs. Sharpe. You can gossip down at the beauty shop if you're bored."

Same old Guttman. He always called her Mrs. Sharpe when he wanted to intimidate her. Well, it wasn't going to work this time. She clicked her pen and started right in on the questions.

"Is it usual to conduct such a shoddy investigation when someone dies in Maycroft?" She braced herself for the blow-back.

Guttman rubbed his forehead as though he had a migraine coming on. "What makes you think it was a shoddy investigation?"

His tone revealed more patience than Deena had expected. "Well, it sounds like Linndorf and his fellow officers concluded that Granger's death was a suicide without much thought to anything else. I thought the police were supposed to assume all suspicious deaths were homicides until proven otherwise."

Guttman nodded slowly. "You hit the nail on the head. All 'suspicious' deaths. This one was open and shut according to the officers. Fingerprints on the gun matched Granger. It was laying right by him."

It was too pat an answer. "I guess you and I have different definitions of the word 'suspicious.' For example, I find it suspicious that a man who just found out his wife was expecting their first child would take his life."

"You do? Haven't you seen some of those bratty kids shows on TV? Like the ones where the parents have to hire a special nanny just to keep from killing their kids? No, thank you. I'd rather have a dog." He took a big swig of coffee.

"Seriously. Did his wife say he was depressed upon hearing the news or was he excited like most men would be?"

"Maybe it wasn't his baby."

"Exactly!" Deena pointed her finger at him. "And wouldn't that be suspicious?"

Guttman shrugged and just stared back.

Deena could feel her temperature start to rise. It wasn't like Guttman to make jokes. He was usually a "just the facts" kind of detective. "I suppose you at least checked out Allison's alibi for the night her husband died."

"She was at her book club. From what I understand, that's code for women getting away from their husbands to drink wine and complain about their coworkers. Am I wrong?"

Deena snorted, but then had to admit he was right. "Okay, but did you talk to the other members of the club at least? Maybe Allison ducked out, went home and shot her husband, drove away and hid out until after the police came. Did you consider that?"

"There was no reason to. Why can't you just accept the facts here, Mrs. Sharpe. Is this because of that news editor, Dan

Carson?" Guttman motioned to Clara for more coffee. "He's always trying to stir up trouble."

As Clara returned and flirted with the detective, Deena looked back at her notes. She couldn't understand why she wasn't getting straight answers for her questions. Was it because she was a woman and he didn't take her seriously? Surely not. She had helped him on cases in the past. Maybe he was covering for somebody.

Clara left without even looking at Deena or filling her cup.

Guttman grinned. "You were saying..."

"Owen Walsh."

"Who?"

"Owen Walsh owns a farm and has a grudge against the Grangers. Maybe you should check him out."

Guttman pulled out an imaginary pencil from behind his ear and pretended to make a note. "Question Owen Walsh, the book club gals, Santa Claus, and the Easter Bunny. Anything else?" He looked up.

Deena wasn't amused. "But what about gunshot residue and the trajectory of the bullet? How about blood splatter or signs of forced entry? What about the whereabouts of his wife and other possible suspects?"

Guttman shook his finger playfully and grinned. "You've been watching television crime shows, haven't you?"

"Yes, and maybe you should, too!" The volume of her statement drew the attention of those nearby.

Clara swung by with the coffeepot and filled Guttman's cup even though he'd barely taken a sip. She put her chubby hand on his shoulder. "Everything okay over here with you and your mother?"

Deena curled her lip and felt light-headed. She glared at Guttman, expecting him to correct the wretched waitress.

Instead, he nodded and said, "We're fine. I think I'll have a blueberry muffin, if it's not too much trouble." He looked across the table. "How about you, Mother?"

"I'll mother *you*," she seethed through pursed lips before realizing how awkward that sounded. She sneered at Clara and said, "I'll have the same."

Guttman smiled. "Like mother, like son."

Clara jotted down the order, stuck the pencil behind her ear, and winked. "I do *loooove* me a mama's boy."

By the time Clara left, Deena had lost her appetite as well as her patience. "You realize she's older than me, right?"

"Maybe I like mature women," Guttman said. "She makes a mean cup of java."

"Stop deflecting, Detective Guttman. I'm a reporter and I'm asking you real questions on the record. I expect straight answers." She could feel the hot flash subsiding into a cold sweat.

"I didn't realize we were on the record." He fidgeted with his beard. "I thought we were just two friends breaking bread and shooting the breeze about current events."

"That flew off the table when you called me 'mother,'" Deena said. "You are the only detective in the Maycroft Police Department. The investigation was your responsibility. So, will you give me a statement or not?"

He avoided eye contact as he fiddled with the creamer.

As a tray of water glasses crashed to the ground, the sound of glass breaking in the kitchen drew everyone's attention. A young waitress and a busboy began pointing fingers as to whose fault it was. Through the clamor, Deena remained motionless and kept her eyes glued on Guttman. She knew he was either hiding something or stalling. She was prepared to wait.

He finally looked back and met her gaze. Reaching in his pocket, he pulled out a twenty-dollar bill and threw it on the table. "This is off the record." He took a big swig of coffee and then leaned in. "The reason I can't answer your questions, Mrs. Sharpe, is because I don't know the answers. I had to rely on the report of my acting investigator, Clay Hitchcock."

"Officer Hitchcock? He used to be Larry Linndorf's partner, right?" She threw out her hands. "So why didn't you follow up?"

Guttman shrugged and stood up. "You see, I was out of town the week Andrew Granger died. He was six feet under by the time I even found out about the case. There was really nothing I could do."

* * *

DEENA COULDN'T WAIT to get home and write up her news story for Monday's paper. She raised the question about the thoroughness of the investigation and said that an anonymous source claimed Andrew Granger may have been murdered, although she left out anything about Edwina and Allison. She emailed the story to Dan, who approved it with a few minor changes. He made her include the part about Hitchcock and Linndorf having been former partners.

"Do you think that implies they were possibly in cahoots?" she asked Dan when he called her.

"It's a fact and it needs to be put out there," he said. "If we want Guttman to reopen the case, there needs to be evidence that the department didn't handle the investigation as they should have. It will be up to the public—and the mayor—to apply pressure."

Deena agreed and made the changes. She was excited to be getting a byline even though the story wouldn't be on the front page. She spent the next few hours organizing her notes and writing questions she still wanted answers for.

When Gary got home, Deena unloaded on him about Guttman. When she finally stopped to take a breath, he squared his shoulders and asked, "Are you telling me that you're the new crime reporter?"

Oops. It was no use. She couldn't keep secrets from her husband. "Yes. Major crime like murders and such. And I'm good at it, too. So, get over it."

He started to speak but closed his mouth, apparently knowing she had made up her mind. Then he asked, "Did you ask Guttman about Allison and whether or not there had been allegations of abuse?"

She smacked her forehead. "I was so rattled I didn't get to ask half my questions." She made herself a note.

Gary pulled out a chair from the kitchen table and sat. "Let me get this straight. There's Allison, who may or may not have been abused and who has been accused by her sister-in-law of killing Drew."

"And she's pregnant, let's not forget," Deena added. "Edwina said Allison was having an affair, so it may not be Drew's baby."

"Right," Gary said, nodding thoughtfully. "Any other suspects?"

Deena paced across the floor. "Owen Walsh, the man who accused Drew of stealing his prized vines and then showed up at the funeral and confronted Allison. When I mentioned his name to Guttman, he acted like he'd never heard of him."

"Anyone else?"

Deena stopped pacing and sat down across from Gary. "I've been giving this a lot of thought. Who else might have benefitted from Drew's death?"

Gary's eyes narrowed. "You can't be serious. I had no idea I was in the will until yesterday."

"Not you, silly! I mean Edwina Granger. She started this whole thing but still hasn't gotten back in touch with me. Doesn't that seem suspicious? As a relative, she might be in the will, too."

"Right." Gary nodded. "Which would give her a motive to accuse Allison."

Hurley barked at Deena, so she put him on her lap. "You mean to take the heat off of herself?"

"Not necessarily. You see, Drew's death creates a conundrum." Gary took on the professorial tone he used when talking about finances. "If Drew committed suicide, then the bulk of his estate, including any life insurance, would most likely go to his wife. That's pretty standard. But if he was murdered and the killer turns out to be Allison, the insurance would probably revert to his next living kin, which would be his sister. Edwina could also sue for the rest of the estate unless Drew had set up a trust for possible children."

"But Allison's his wife."

"No insurance company is going to pay out to a man's killer." He raised his eyebrows. "That's something for you to remember in case you ever decide to get rid of me."

Deena ignored the comment as she contemplated this new twist. "So, Edwina Granger could have killed her brother and blamed it on Allison to try to get her hands on the entire estate."

"That's right."

Deena looked down at Hurley and rubbed his ears. "You know, there's one other suspect we haven't talked about. The man's best friend."

Gary shot her a look. "Man's best friend? You mean a dog?"

Deena laughed as she set Hurley back down. For someone so smart, Gary definitely had his "blond" moments. "No, Drew's best friend. Lonnie Fisher."

"You're kidding, right?" Gary stood up and shoved his hands in his pockets. "Do you really suspect Lonnie?"

"I can't put my finger on it. There's something about him that strikes me as suspicious. Maybe he thought he could get his hands on the vineyard with Drew out of the picture. Maybe that's why Allison didn't like him. She might have had her own suspicions. Women have a way of knowing things. That is, unless they were having an affair—like you said—and then all bets are off."

Gary shook his head as he walked into the kitchen and came out with one of the bottles of wine Lonnie had given him. He held it close as though for security. "I think you're barking up the wrong tree. Lonnie and Drew were close. Like brothers, almost."

"I've got two words for you," Deena said as she crossed her arms. "Cain and Abel."

Chapter 16

GARY WAS NERVOUS AS a cat when they pulled up to the Lyons and Sons law offices at a minute past nine on Monday morning. They had been held up from getting there on time by Christy Ann, their neighbor. She had stopped Deena in the driveway to ask her about the article in the morning's newspaper about Andrew Granger's death. It was obvious Christy Ann was curious about any salacious gossip she could spread.

Deena had secretly enjoyed having the upper hand as she kept tight-lipped about additional details and told her nosy neighbor to keep her eye on the next edition if she wanted to know more of the story.

"I hate being late," Gary mumbled as he scooted out of the car. "It's so unprofessional."

"Hold your water. You're a guest, not the host of this shindig," Deena said. "Take a breath and remember to keep your eye on the prize. We're trying to weed out the bad apple from the Granger family orchard."

"Sure, but don't go all Perry Mason on these people. Show some decorum."

Deena feigned insult. "Who, me? I *reek* of decorum."

They headed inside where the receptionist led them to a large conference room.

Allison Granger sat next to her attorney. "What is *she* doing here?" She turned her nose up at Deena.

Allison wore a drab gray suit along with a sour expression. The only resemblance to the merry widow from the funeral was her bright red lips and dangly chandelier earrings.

"This is my wife, Deena," Gary said by way of excuse for the intrusion. "She's with me." He smiled weakly hoping Allison wouldn't throw them both out.

"I know who she is." She turned to Deena. "I read that piece of trash in today's newspaper. I thought you were writing a tribute to Drew. Instead, you smeared his name by implying someone hated him enough to kill him. How dare you show your face here."

Eric Lyons III rose from the brown leather chair at the end of the long conference table and stood next to Allison. It was obvious where his allegiance lay. "Mr. Sharpe, please take a seat at the table. Your wife can wait in the reception area."

Deena shot a look to her husband, who returned it with a helpless shrug of his shoulders. Deena wasn't leaving without a fight. "Allison, I never said that Andrew was murdered. I just pointed out how little the Maycroft Police Department did in investigating the possibility. I would think you, of all people, would want to know for sure what happened to your husband while you were at your 'book club.'"

"How did you know where I was?" Allison stopped abruptly. She glared at Deena, then said, "Fine," and whispered something to her attorney.

Lyons looked at his watch. "We'll give the others a few more minutes and then get started."

Deena started to ask who else was supposed to be there, but a swift kick under the table by Gary made her close her mouth and sit quietly. It was for the best. She didn't want to press her luck with Allison or Gary.

Deena glanced around at the elaborately decorated conference room. The mahogany table looked as though it could seat the entire royal family and then some. Oil paintings of Eric Lyons junior and senior decorated the walls along with several pieces of taxidermy. The deer, moose, and fowl looked like they were ready to storm the place if anyone got out of line. She stared into the moose's eyes, wondering if they concealed a hidden camera.

Maybe Guttman was right. Perhaps she *had* been watching too many crime shows.

The door opened and Lonnie Fisher appeared all decked out in an expensive charcoal-gray suit with a pink-and-gray-striped tie with a matching pocket square. Deena could see the admiration on Gary's face and was sure he would ask about Lonnie's tailor before the two left.

Lonnie shook hands with Gary, while Deena kept her hands in her lap, not wanting a repeat of the previous painful handshake. Lonnie gave Allison and her attorney a slight wave and head nod before taking a seat across the table from the Sharpes, leaving an empty seat between himself and Allison.

Lyons had returned to his throne at the head of the table and opened a black leather portfolio to reveal a thick document.

Deena grinned, knowing that at three hundred dollars an hour this affair was probably costing Allison a fortune. Served her right for not granting Deena an interview.

Lyons glanced at his watch again. "We should get started even though Edwina Granger has not arrived. I never received confirmation that she was coming."

"I doubt she'll show up," Allison said. "She wasn't at the funeral and hasn't been seen or heard around these parts in years."

Again, Deena started to speak and felt the nudge of Gary's foot. It was all she could do not to blurt out that she'd received a visit from Edwina just a few days earlier. Deena hoped like heck that Edwina would come through the door any minute and throw Allison Granger into a tailspin. Maybe that would knock a confession out of her.

Lyons cleared his throat and started in with some legal gibberish that Deena did her best to tune out. She couldn't get the meeting with Edwina out of her head. The woman had seemed so certain that Allison was responsible for Andrew's death. Why wouldn't she have contacted Detective Guttman about the investigation? Why hadn't she gotten back in touch with Deena?

And just like that, the door opened again, and there was Edwina Granger. She wore the same floral dress and worn-out shoes she had on when she visited Deena at her office.

"Sorry I'm late, Mr. Lyons. My car wouldn't start." She glared at Allison. "I suppose you are Andrew's widow."

"Yes, I'm Allison." She stood and approached the other woman. "I'm glad to finally meet you." Allison extended her arms as if to offer a hug.

Edwina took a step back and started toward a seat at the table. She gasped as she caught sight of Deena. "Oh, Mrs. Sharpe. I didn't expect to see you here." She awkwardly sat down and scooted her chair away from Deena.

"You two know each other?" Allison asked in surprise.

"Yes, we've recently met," Deena said. She smiled sweetly at Edwina as though they shared recipes and did each other's nails.

Deena noticed Lonnie Fisher eyeing the woman suspiciously. Had the two of them ever met? She shuffled the facts in her brain and tried to remember what Lonnie had said. She didn't recall him mentioning Edwina, and the woman didn't seem to acknowledge his presence.

Lyons cleared his throat again and continued. "Let's get to it. Mr. Sharpe, it was Andrew Granger's will to gift you with a case each of his three favorite wines in appreciation of your service and kindness in matters of financial interest. They will be delivered to your home after probate."

Gary's eyes lit up. "How kind. Drew was such a thoughtful man." He smiled at Allison, who nodded back.

Deena wondered if Gary was disappointed. Had he secretly hoped to get a percentage of the winery? Surely not. Looking at Gary, he seemed perfectly satisfied.

Lyons slid an envelope toward Lonnie. "Mr. Fisher, it was Mr. Granger's will to leave you this gold ring in appreciation for your hard work and friendship. Mrs. Granger was kind enough to bring it here today."

Lonnie squeezed the envelope and slipped it inside the breast pocket of his suit jacket.

"He just loved that ring," Allison said, "almost as much as his wedding band. I hope you appreciate it."

"I do," Lonnie said, wiping a tear from his eye.

An awkward silence followed as the attorney found the page of the will he needed next. He looked to Allison. "Well, that was the easy part. This next part is complicated...and personal. Would you like for Mr. Sharpe and Mr. Fisher to be excused?"

Allison looked surprised. "Is it about the vineyard?"

"Yes," Lyons answered curtly.

Deena's stomach churned. This was the part she'd been waiting for. If Allison asked them to leave now, she'd miss all the information that might prove a motive for Allison to kill her husband.

"Well," Allison said slowly, "Gary handles all our finances and Lonnie is currently running the business, so I guess they'll find out the details eventually anyway. It's probably best if they stay." She shot a sour look at Edwina.

Deena breathed easy and tried her best to look uninterested.

"In that case, I'll skip the legal details and get to the facts. As you may or may not know—"

The conference room door swung open again and the receptionist shot her boss a confused look. A woman flew in past her, looking flushed under her tanned complexion. Her long sandy-brown hair was pulled back in a ponytail and braided. She wore jeans and a colorful Aztec fleece jacket over a white cotton blouse. Her western boots scuffed across the thick carpet as she hurried over to Eric Lyons.

She shot out her hand. "I'm so sorry I'm late. The plane had to circle the airport and then there was the Dallas traffic. I got here as soon as I could." She glanced around the table as everyone stared at her curiously.

Lyons stood, returned the handshake, and said, "Please forgive me, but who are you?"

The woman seemed astonished. "I'm Nina Davenport. You sent me a letter." Then locking eyes with Allison, she added, "I'm Andrew's sister."

Chapter 17

OVER THE NEXT FEW MOMENTS, they all looked like spectators at a tennis match as everyone glanced back and forth from one woman to the other. It was like an old episode of the game show *To Tell the Truth* as the panel waited for the real Edwina Granger to "please stand up."

Finally, the first Edwina blurted out, "That's impossible! *I'm* Andrew's sister."

The woman who had introduced herself as Nina Davenport looked startled. "What are you talking about? I'm Edwina Granger Davenport. *You* must be an imposter."

Allison's hands flew up to her face. "What's happening here?"

Lyons patted her shoulder. "Allison, surely you can identify your brother's sister for us."

She shook her head. "I can't. We've never met. The only pictures I've seen are from when she and Drew were kids."

Deena couldn't sit quietly anymore. "This is the woman who came to my office saying she was Edwina Granger." She touched the arm of the woman sitting next to her. "Although now that I think about it, I didn't get any proof."

"Proof? You want proof?" Nina opened her handbag and pulled out her billfold. She removed her driver's license and shoved it at Deena. "Here's my ID."

Deena took it. "This is from Nevada."

"That's where I live." She snatched it back from Deena and handed it to the attorney.

Lyons studied it and said, "Looks legit to me." He arched an eyebrow as everyone looked back at the first Edwina. The ball was now in her court.

"This is ridiculous!" Now under the microscope, she opened her handbag and shut it quickly. Her face drained of color. "I changed purses before I came and must have left my identification in my other bag."

No one was buying her story.

She stood up. "Let me just step out and make a phone call. I'll have my husband bring it here." She left the room in a hurry.

Deena whispered to Gary that she was going to find the ladies' room and walked out before he could protest.

Once outside in the hallway, she headed toward the lobby. The first Edwina was huddled in the corner talking on her cell phone. Deena moved a few steps closer and stood behind a tall fern and tried to appear nonchalant.

The receptionist stared at her suspiciously, so Deena pulled out her own phone as though she too were making a call.

"You said I wouldn't get caught," Edwina seethed into her phone. "What am I supposed to do now?"

Deena could hardly believe it. This woman was only pretending to be Edwina Granger. Deena had been duped. Not only that, but the whole idea that Allison killed her husband was probably a ruse, and she had fallen for it. Before she could feel too guilty about the pain she had caused Allison, the other woman put her phone back in her purse. Deena dashed back around the corner before she could be seen. As she reentered the conference room, she debated what to do. Should she expose the woman as a fraud or wait and see what she did? Maybe she would take off and never show her face here again.

But as sure as the sun rises in the east, the fake Edwina walked back in with her head high and her shoulders back. "My husband will have to take off work to bring over my identification. It may be a while." She took her seat.

"I don't want to wait," Allison groaned. "Let's just get this over with, and we'll sort out who's who later."

Lyons motioned for "Edwina" to take a seat by Lonnie Fisher. "If you'll be seated, Mrs. Davenport, I suppose we will continue."

"Please, call me Nina." She sat across the table from her counterpart, who strategically avoided eye contact.

Now that Deena knew the real Edwina from the fake one, she wanted to watch the imposter's reaction to the contents of Andrew's will. Maybe she could figure out what her motive might have been to embark on this charade in the first place. Deena would tell Lyons what she'd just overheard when the time was right.

"Let me see," the attorney said, looking back at the stack of documents. "Where was I?"

"You had just said that this was about to get complicated." Deena shot him a sly grin.

He looked over the top of his glasses and glanced between the two Edwinas. "Yes, I remember." He turned to Allison. "As you know, Edward Granger started Granger's Grapes in the

1980s. My father was his attorney then. From my understanding, Andrew and his sister began working at the vineyard in their teens. You—one of you—is a few years older than Andrew."

"Two years older," the real Edwina said.

The fake one said, "That's right."

Shaking his head, Lyons continued. "Then, when Andrew turned twenty-one, Mr. Granger turned over the full operation to his two children. However, something occurred a few years later that resulted in his removing his daughter from the management of the business and cutting her out of his will. He put the ownership of the company in a trust for Andrew, stating that he would own it full and clear upon his thirty-fifth birthday."

Allison gasped. "But Andrew just turned thirty-three. What does that mean?" Her eyes almost burst from their sockets.

"This is where it gets tricky," Lyons said. "You see, Mr. Granger, the father, was a very religious man. Apparently, that's why he cut you"—he looked at the two women—"or you, out of his will. It is my understanding that because of some indiscretion, he decided to put a morality clause in his will that Andrew would take possession of the business as long as he committed no 'moral imprudence' by the time he reached age thirty-five." Lyons read that last part straight from the paper he held in his hand.

"That shouldn't be a problem," Allison said, her face relaxing back to normal. "Andrew was a good man."

This time, it was Nina—the real sister—who scoffed. "Whatever."

Allison's claws came out. "What are you saying? How would you even know? You haven't even spoken to Drew in years. That is, if you really are his sister."

"She's not," the fake Edwina said.

Deena thought it might be time to set the record straight, but Lyons interrupted. "Ladies! Please refrain from comment until I have finished."

They all shut their mouths and listened.

"As I was saying, Mr. Granger made a list of what he considered to be moral indiscretions, including things like committing murder, adultery, and theft. Unfortunately, on the list is suicide."

That brought a collective gasp from the group.

Before anyone could say anything, Lyons added, "As you all know, Andrew's death was ruled a suicide. Therefore, the ownership of the entire business—Granger's Grapes, Inc.—goes to his closest blood relative. In this case, that would be his sister, Edwina Granger."

The fake sister clapped her hands and let out a loud "Whoop!"

Nina's jaw dropped as she stared at Lyons.

Allison lowered her head and began to cry into her wad of tissues.

It was time to call out the fraud. Deena stood and asked Lyons to join her by the door. Looking helpless to relieve his client's distress, he got up and followed her. Deena told him what she had overheard as well as how Edwina the First had accused Allison of murder.

His eyes narrowed as he nodded his understanding. He walked over to the fake sister and whispered something in her ear.

She leaped from her seat clutching her purse. "How dare you accuse me of fraud! We'll see who's a fraud!"

"Perhaps you'd like to explain that to the police. I'm sure they'll be happy to sort this all out for us. Although, I believe the penalty for fraud and perjury carries a good deal of jail time."

"Jail!" she shouted, wide-eyed. "I'm not going to jail for this. That creep Woody Davenport should be the one going to jail. Not me." She raced from the room.

"Should I follow her?" Deena asked anxiously.

"No," Gary and Lyons said simultaneously.

Lyons added, "I doubt we'll ever see her again." He turned to Nina. "Have you ever heard of a man named Woody Davenport?"

She rolled her eyes. "Of course. He's my husband."

"I CAN'T BELIEVE IT!" Allison moaned. "That snake went and killed himself knowing full well that he was leaving me destitute. And after all I did for him and put up with."

"Perhaps we should discuss this in private, Allison." Lyons motioned toward the door. "Would you like to come back to my office?"

Allison shook her head. "Not if it's going to cost me more money. Now I'm not going to be able to pay you. That stupid Andrew."

Nina eyed Allison. "That was a fast change of heart. At least now you see him for the conman he really was."

"Shut up," Allison said. "You have no right to talk about him that way. Besides, it seems to me if your father cut you out of his will, you shouldn't get to inherit the business anyway. Right, Eric? Can we sue her or something?"

He cleared his throat. "There are a number of ways to challenge probate. We can discuss those at another time."

Deena wondered why he was being coy with Allison. Maybe he was hoping to bag the now-rich Edwina Granger Davenport as a new client. Then Deena remembered something. "What about the baby?"

Allison's face turned three shades of purple. "What?"

"Mr. Lyons said the inheritance would go to Andrew's closest relative, right? Since you're pregnant, maybe your unborn child is first in line." Deena expected Allison to jump for joy; instead she just stared back with her mouth ajar.

"You're expecting?" Lyons knitted his brow. "You never mentioned that."

Allison sucked in a deep breath. "That's because I'm not."

Gary shot daggers at Deena, then said, "I think we should be going."

Deena remained seated. "But—but—you said—"

Allison cut her off. "I don't know what you're talking about, Mrs. Sharpe, and neither do you." She turned back to her lawyer. "Andrew couldn't stand his sister, and I'd rather anyone else get the winery than her. Are you sure there's not a loophole in there somewhere that would block this?"

Nina's face turned smug for the first time. "I didn't even want the business...until now."

Lyons, trying to avoid a family feud or catfight or worse, pulled Allison up by the arm. "Let's discuss this in my office."

"I'm not a child," she said, shaking his hand loose from her arm. "Besides, how do we even know Andrew actually did commit suicide? Mrs. Sharpe thinks he was murdered. She said so right there in the *Tribune*."

Before Deena could protest again, Lyons was pushing Allison out of the conference room. Over her shoulder, Allison called out, "Deena, I'll be in touch."

Chapter 18

THE SHARPES, EDWINA Granger, and Lonnie Fisher all sat in stunned silence, not sure of what to do next.

"Well," Gary finally said, "I guess we should leave."

Just then the receptionist stuck her head in to say Mr. Lyons would contact them as soon as he had more information to share. She asked Edwina to stop by the front desk to leave her contact number.

Gary leaned across the table. "Lonnie, nice to see you again." They shook hands.

"Maybe I'll see you sometime in the future, unless I end up moving back to Dallas. Who knows if I still have a job after today." He looked over at Deena. "And you, Mrs. Sharpe, I certainly hope you are not seriously planning to follow that ridiculous claim that Drew was murdered. It would be a shame to smear such a good man's name when he's not here to defend himself."

Deena started to say something when Edwina interrupted. "Mr. Fisher, is it? You obviously didn't know the same Andrew Granger that I grew up with. The Andrew I knew—"

"You're right, Mrs. Davenport. I didn't know the man you described as a conman. It's too bad you didn't know the Drew

115

that I worked side by side with all these years. People can change, you know. We aren't just stuck in one place our whole lives. Have you ever thought that maybe you and your family caused your brother's problems when he was younger?" Without waiting for a response, Lonnie stormed out of the conference room.

Edwina glared as he rushed by her. "It's obvious Drew pulled the wool over his eyes." She picked up her handbag. "Sorry if I was rude, Mrs. Sharpe. It's been a rough couple of days. I had no idea that woman was trying to pass herself off as me."

"I completely understand," Deena said as she got up and stood by Gary. "I'm sure you're exhausted and confused and...thrilled."

"Thrilled?" Edwina narrowed her eyes. "Why on earth would I be thrilled?"

Deena ignored Gary's throat clearing. "Because you just inherited the winery. I'm sure it will make you a rich woman."

"Oh, that." Edwina walked around the table toward the door. "I'm sure I'll never see a penny of that. Allison will do everything in her power to keep it out of my hands. Frankly, she can have it for all I care."

Why on earth would she say that? Was she already wealthy? The rich never act like they care about money. Deena was determined to find out what the woman's story was. "Nina, where are you staying? Do you need a ride? We'd be happy to give you a lift."

Her face softened. "I have a rental car, but thanks. Actually, I thought I might be getting an invitation to stay with Allison. Obviously, that's out of the question."

"You're welcome to stay with us. Right, Gary?"

His face was a mixture of surprise and worry. "Um, sure. Although there are a number of charming bed and breakfast places in Maycroft that you might enjoy."

Nina chuckled. "Don't worry, Mr. Sharpe. I'm not going to invade your home. I appreciate the offer though."

Deena followed Nina into the lobby. "Well, at least let us buy you lunch."

Nina shook her head. "Thanks, but I'm really tired. I just want to find a place to crash and get my thoughts together. By the way, do you know where Drew was buried? I'd like to visit his grave."

Deena glanced at Gary, hoping he wouldn't blow her cover. "Actually, I do. I can take you there. Why don't we meet at the Café Hut on Main in about an hour, and I'll take you to the cemetery?"

Maybe Nina wanted some company or maybe Deena had just worn her down, but either way Nina agreed.

After she left, Deena pulled Gary's arm back toward the receptionist's desk.

"What are you doing?" he asked.

"I've got to talk to Allison before we leave."

"Why?"

"I have to find out where she buried her husband."

Chapter 19

ANXIOUSLY DRUMMING her fingers on the table, Deena watched as car after car drove by the coffee shop without pulling in. Why hadn't she gotten Nina's cell phone number? For all she knew, Nina Davenport could be on her way back to Nevada, and Deena would be left with a million unanswered questions.

On the other hand, at least she wouldn't have to admit to lying to the woman's face. Not only had she not known where Drew Granger was buried, she also didn't realize that Allison was still in possession of his ashes. Deena had gotten that bit of information before leaving the attorney's office.

She debated calling Dan and catching him up on the latest developments when she saw Nina pull into the parking lot. Deena gulped down the end of her mocha latte and put on her best concerned-friend face.

Nina waved, ordered a coffee, and joined Deena at the table. "Thanks for waiting," she said. "I didn't have your number to let you know I was going to be late. I took a room at the Wisteria Inn and Mrs. Swanson felt the need to explain the whole history of the property, including how to properly flush the toilet."

Deena laughed. "The Swansons go to our church. She's a real talker, that's for sure. But she makes a mean sausage gravy and biscuit though, so it will be worth it."

Nina nodded slowly and eyed Deena cautiously. "I realize that you are a reporter, but I hope you aren't just trying to get information for a story out of me."

The guilt was too much for Deena to brush off. "Actually, that's part of it. I would be lying to say otherwise. But you need to know your brother was a client and friend of Gary's, and we both really care about what happened to him. From what I have discovered, there were no signs that he was depressed to the point of taking his own life. Yes, I'm writing a story for the newspaper, but the end goal is to be sure there is justice if some-one did something to Drew."

Nina stared over her coffee cup out the window as Deena held her breath. She was hoping Nina wouldn't jump up and take off like a scared rabbit.

At last she said, "Fair enough. But before we head out to the cemetery, I want to ask you about the imposter who was claiming to be me and what involvement my husband may have had in their little scheme."

Relieved, Deena started from the beginning. "You see, over the past few years, I've been involved in investigating a few murder cases around here. It began with my uncle's cold case and just spread from there. I guess I've developed a reputation for finding killers."

"Unusual hobby."

She shrugged. "Some people knit. I sleuth. Anyway, a woman came to me claiming to be you. She said her brother was murdered and that she thought Allison had done it."

"That doesn't surprise me. If Woody was involved, he'd be looking to get Allison out of the picture."

"There's more," Deena added, wishing she hadn't finished her coffee so quickly. "She said Allison was having an affair. I don't know if that's true or not, although Lonnie Fisher confirmed that Drew and Allison hadn't been 'intimate' lately."

Nina wrinkled her nose. "That's an awfully private detail for a man to share with his coworker, don't you think? I can't imagine Drew would have said that to anyone."

"I know what you mean, but apparently the two were close. Lonnie said they were like brothers."

Nina scoffed. "That's what Drew said about Woody after we got married, and you know how that turned out."

"Actually, I don't. What happened with you and your brother?"

Nina sat back. "I'll tell you, but only if it's off the record and only if we get more coffee."

"Deal." Deena fetched them each a second cup and they moved to a table in the far corner to avoid the early lunch crowd that would soon fill the small shop.

Nina doctored her coffee with cream and artificial sugar while Deena spooned heaps of whipped cream into her mouth. Maybe she would have Nina's trim figure if she'd skipped the mocha and sugar, but then life really wouldn't be worth living.

"Woody Davenport and I got married right after we graduated high school. I went to college and got an associate's degree in accounting. I was too impatient to spend four years in college just to end up working in my father's business. Woody already working in the production end of the company when

Drew and I both started working there full-time. I was the money manager; Drew was in charge of marketing and sales."

"Quite the family business." Although the arrangement sounded cozy, she could also see it had the potential for problems.

"Things rocked along just fine for a few years until my father became ill, that is, and stepped out of the day-to-day operation. He made Drew the CEO and me the chief financial officer. I was fine with that. Woody and I were hoping to start a family and Drew was still single, so it made sense."

"I have a feeling there's a 'but' coming," Deena said.

"Yep. The company was starting to make money, but expenses seemed out of whack. It didn't take long for me to figure out that Drew and Woody had pulled the wool over my eyes. They were inflating expenses and pocketing the profit. I was stunned. Not only that, but I was caught between a rock and a hard place. I couldn't turn a blind eye to the whole thing and cheat my father, you know?"

"Of course not. But what did you do?"

Nina sipped her coffee. "I thought I was doing the right thing. I'd do it again today if I had to." She sucked in a deep breath. "I ratted them out to my father."

Deena shook her head. "That was incredibly brave and responsible of you." Her opinion of Nina Davenport kicked up about three notches. "Is that what caused the big fallout between you and Drew?"

"Yes, but it gets worse. You see, my brother denied any involvement in the scheme. He blamed it on Woody and me."

"Oh no," Deena said as her hand flew to her mouth. "You're kidding."

"I wish I were. Since I was in charge of the bookkeeping, it was easy for my father to blame me. And since he had never really cottoned to Woody, he and I got all the blame. That's when Daddy disowned me and turned over everything to Drew. I heard he got married shortly after that."

"No wonder you and your brother were estranged all these years." Deena couldn't imagine being in Nina's shoes. She was close to her own brother, Russell, and would be lost without him. She remembered something else. "Is that why your father put the clause in his will about Drew living a sin-free life?"

"I suppose so." Nina stirred her half-empty cup, creating a miniature tornado. "This morning was the first I'd heard about it. I doubt Drew knew about it either. Of course, the irony is that the terms of the will mean that everything reverted back to me anyway. Daddy would be rolling over in his grave if he knew that." A few tears slipped down her cheeks.

Deena handed her a wad of napkins from the dispenser. "I'm so sorry. Family issues can be complicated." She didn't know what else to say.

Nina dabbed her eyes. "What makes it even more crazy is that I don't think Drew really killed himself. If it turns out that someone else killed him, I lose the family business and it all goes to Allison."

"Unless Allison killed him," Deena added.

"Do you really think she might have?"

Deena didn't want to expose all the cards in her hand. After all, she'd just met this woman. She didn't want to tell her about the possible physical abuse, the sketchy book club alibi, or the pregnancy hoax until she found out more about Edwina

Granger Davenport. However, her first impression was that the woman seemed honest and everything she said made sense.

"Tell me about your husband, Woody Davenport," Deena said. "How do you think he is involved in this?"

Nina's eyes went from weepy to worried. "You heard that woman say that he was behind her scam. I wouldn't put it past him to do something to get revenge on Drew and his hands on the family money."

The coffee shop began filling up as Deena had suspected. It was getting harder to keep their conversation private. She waved to a couple of people she knew as they glanced suspiciously at the stranger with whom she was sitting.

"Maybe we should go somewhere more private," Deena suggested.

"How about the cemetery? I can follow you."

Deena's mouth went dry. "Why don't you let me drive you? I can drop you back here afterwards; that way we can talk in the car where it is warmer." If she trapped Nina in her car, she'd be a captive audience when she confessed to lying about knowing where Drew was buried.

"Okay," Nina sighed. "Are we going to Restful Pines? That's where Daddy is buried."

"Yes," Deena said quickly. "Restful Pines it is." If nothing else, Nina would be able to visit her father's gravesite while they were there. It wouldn't be a complete waste of time.

Deena headed to the highway that led just out of town to the cemetery. "Does Woody live with you in Nevada?"

"Oh heavens, no," Nina said. "He lives just west of here. We separated shortly after my father fired us. That was about eleven years ago. Neither of us bothered to file for divorce. I guess that means Woody never found someone else to settle down with either."

Deena drove just under the speed limit, taking her time to reach their destination. "What about you? What have you been doing all this time?"

"I wandered here and there for a while until I stumbled upon this boys ranch near Lake Tahoe. They were looking for someone to be a house parent who also knew how to handle horses. We grew up with horses, so I applied and got the job. It didn't take me long to fall in love with the place. I went to school part-time to become a licensed counselor. Now I do social work with troubled boys."

"Like your brother?"

Nina dropped her eyes. "The people I work with don't know what happened with Drew and I. But yes, I think I was drawn to helping these boys because I wasn't able to reestablish a relationship with my brother."

Deena glanced over and saw tears welling in Nina's eyes again.

"In the back of my mind, I think I was practicing on them for when I would get to try again with my brother. But now it's too late. I'll never get that chance."

A lump caught in Deena's throat. Her heart went out to Nina as she realized the woman was just another victim of a tragic event. She pulled into the entrance of Restful Pines and parked just inside the gate. Her maternal instincts kicked in. Yes, she had them even though she had never borne her own children.

"I'm so sorry, dear. You couldn't have known this would happen."

Nina nodded. "I tried, but I should have tried harder."

Time to bite the bullet. "I have my own confession to make," Deena said slowly. "I lied about your brother being buried here. The truth is that he was cremated and Allison still has his ashes."

"Really?" Surprisingly, Nina's eyes lit up. "That means I might be able to get some from her. A woman I work with keeps some of her husband's ashes in a special necklace. She says it makes her feel closer to him to keep him near her heart. I wonder if Allison would agree to give me some of his ashes."

Relieved, Deena found herself volunteering to ask. "She said she would be in touch with me soon. I'll see what she says."

"Thank you. Now can we drive over to where my father is buried?"

Deena followed Nina's directions and waited in the car while her new friend spent several minutes alone by her father's grave. It was a beautiful spot even though the grass had yellowed for the winter. Tall pines sent a sweet smell and cast a long shadow across the lawn. It really was a restful resting place.

When Nina got back in the car, she was like a new woman, determined to find out the truth. "We need a plan to get Woody to confess to his part in the plot to scam Allison. He might have killed Drew, or he might have tried to frame Allison after he found out my brother was dead. Either way, we have to figure out what he did and bust him."

This was right up Deena's alley. "Do you know how to find him? If so, I have an idea."

"Perfect," Nina said. "If I know Woody, he's not going to go down without a fight. The sooner we get to him the better. Once a conman, always a conman."

Chapter 20

GARY INSISTED ON GOING with Deena Saturday to see her brother, Russell, and pick up the little toy he had made her. Russell and Estelle lived in the "old money" part of Maycroft on the huge Fitzhugh estate. According to Russell, it was more of a burden to own all that property than a boon, and he often tried to convince Estelle to sell it.

It wasn't like Gary to be so interested in one of Deena's cases, and she wondered if he was worried about her being in danger. He had gone to the gym to get in his workout before Deena woke up, and he was dressed and ready to go when her alarm sounded.

As they pulled down the long driveway beside the stately Fitzhugh Manor, Deena had finally consumed enough coffee to clear her head. "Why are you wanting to be involved in this case? Surely you are not worried about me being in danger? No one has threatened me or followed me or anything this time."

Gary parked around the back of the house—a place reserved for family. He let out a deep breath. "I don't know. I guess I'm restless. It's better than staying home and watching basketball all day."

Deena nearly blew coffee out her nose. If there was one thing that she knew competed with her for Gary's love, it was sports. Make that two things...sports and his mother. "I'm worried about you. I've never seen you like this." She put the back of her hand on his forehead. "No fever." They got out of the car and walked to the back door.

"I'm fine. I just have some things to figure out." His eyes scanned the acreage behind the house. "This is a beautiful piece of property, isn't it? Shame that no one gets to enjoy it."

Like Deena, her brother didn't have any children either. But his reason was because he and Estelle had found each other so late in life.

Estelle opened the door and gave air kisses to her in-laws. "*Bonjour, madame and monsieur,*" she said with a Texas twang and waved them inside. She was wearing a small black beret and a short plaid skirt.

Deena worried they had caught the couple in some sort of role-playing activity. She could have sworn Russell said to be there at eight o'clock.

Gary was clueless. "What's with the getup? Going to a costume party?"

"No, we're going to Paris!" Estelle grinned and clapped her hands. "I'm practicing up on my French. I studied it in school but can barely remember a thing. You should hear Russell try to speak it. He puts the funniest Texas twist on everything."

Relieved, Deena took off her jacket. "I can't believe you were able to convince Russell to leave the country. He hates flying."

"I know, but he loves me so much that he's doing it for me."

Just then Russell, followed by his dog, Maggie, came into the kitchen where they were all standing by the large oak kitchen table.

"*Ahh*, there's my sweet brother now." She gave him double air kisses. "I hear you're jetting off to Europe soon. You'll have so much fun."

"If you say so." He scratched the dog's head. "I'd rather stay here."

Gary crossed his arms. "Russ, have you ever thought about planting something on this land?"

"Like what? Cotton? Corn?"

"I was thinking of something more fun. Like grapes."

"Huh?"

Deena put her hand on her husband's shoulder. "Gary has decided he wants to be a farmer."

"Not a farmer," he protested. "A vintner."

Russell's eyes widened. "Like Andrew Granger? He owned a vineyard and look what happened to him."

Gary shook his head. "What does one thing have to do with another? Besides, wouldn't it be great to work with the land? Build something from scratch? Get your hands dirty?"

All three of them smirked.

Gary held up his hands. "I know, I know. I like my hands clean. And my clothes. And my life. But now that I'm older, I'm ready to do something different." He frowned at them. "I mean, if Russell can fly off to France, surely I can plant a few vines."

Russell slapped Gary's back. "Of course you can, bro. You just say the word and I'll have a John Deere over here in a heartbeat. If we're going to be partners, we'll have to agree on a name."

"Russell!" Deena scolded. "Don't encourage him. He's only got a few more years until retirement. You two can play Old MacDonald all you want after that. You can even buy cows and chickens if you want."

Russell winked at Gary and shrugged his shoulders. "You heard the boss lady. Oh, and that reminds me. Will you keep Maggie for us while we're gone?"

"Sure, but I thought Cliff usually kept her when you traveled."

"Cliff and Rosemary are going with us. He's going to pop the question when they are at the Eiffel Tower."

Deena smiled from ear to ear. "So, the two oldest bachelors in Maycroft are both going to be hitched," she said. "I'm so happy for him."

Russell held up a finger to his lips. "Don't tell anybody. It's a secret. You know how the gossip mill is around here."

Deena nodded. "You can say that again. Like Andrew Granger's murder. After that one article in the paper, the whole town's calling for an investigation."

Russell led them to the parlor-turned-man cave. "Here it is," he said, and held up a small device. "I took a tape recorder and rewired it to pick up external sound with this earbud. It's the best I could do on such short notice."

Estelle beamed. "Isn't Russell a mechanical genius? It works well, too. We practiced secretly taping each other." Her eyes suddenly narrowed as she turned to her husband. "You remembered to erase that, didn't you?"

He chuckled and his face turned red. "Yes. Don't worry. Anyway, you can attach this to your waist and then string the wire up under your jacket. Pin it as high up to your face as you can without letting it show."

Deena took the device and nodded. "Okay, but I won't be the one wearing it. Nina Davenport will have it on when she talks to her husband. We're going to try to get him to confess to murdering his brother-in-law, Andrew Granger."

Concern clouded her brother's face.

She put a finger to her lips. "And don't tell anybody. It's a secret."

Chapter 21

NINA HAD MANAGED TO track down Woody's phone number through some old friends. They agreed to meet at noon at the Texas Tea & Tap Room on the outskirts of town. It had been one of their favorite haunts back in the old days.

The place wouldn't be as crowded at lunchtime, so Deena and Gary planned to hide in a corner at the bar while Nina had lunch with Woody in the dining area. They wanted to be able to keep their eyes on her if something unusual happened. It was unlikely that Woody would recognize Deena or Gary from their one brief encounter at the funeral luncheon, but they didn't want to chance it.

They met up with Nina about a half hour before her designated rendezvous with Woody. Deena and Nina huddled in the restroom while Nina put on the recording device.

Deena pinned the microphone to Nina's sweater. "How did Woody sound on the phone when you talked to him?"

"He was shocked to hear from me. At least that's how he acted." She pulled her jacket back on. "He had to know I was in town after the incident with the fake 'me' at the attorney's office." She zipped up the front of her jacket. "How do I look?"

Deena adjusted the collar to make sure the makeshift microphone was hidden. "Looks perfect."

Nina turned on the machine. "Testing one, two, three." She hit the playback button and heard her voice repeated.

Deena took a step back to admire their handiwork. Nina was an attractive woman who deserved better than Woody Davenport. Perhaps after this whole case was closed, she'd talk to Nina about getting a divorce and finding Mr. Right.

There was a knock on the door to the restroom. It was Gary. "Let's go, ladies. Woody could be here any minute."

Deena nodded and looked back at Nina. "Are you feeling good about our strategy?"

"Definitely. If Woody believes I'm in on his scheme, I'll have him eating out of my hand."

"Okay then. Good luck." Deena gave Nina a quick hug. "It's showtime."

They both hurried to their respective posts—Deena to the bar with Gary, and Nina to a small table in a back corner of the dining room.

Deena recognized Woody right away as he came through the door. She turned around to face the big screen TV above the bar. "This is it," she whispered to Gary. "Time to catch a spider in our web."

* * *

AS WOODY WALKED OVER, Nina switched on the recorder. She forced a smile. Her husband hadn't aged all that well. When he took off his cowboy hat, she saw a deeply receding hairline and wrinkles on his forehead where there used to be none. She wondered if he would think the same thing about her. Then she chided herself for even giving a moment's thought to what a creep like Woody would think about her.

"Hey, darlin'." He said it as though they'd only been apart ten minutes instead of ten years. "How have you been?"

"Fine, sugar. And you?"

"Better now that you're back."

She started to protest that she had no intention of being "back," but stopped herself. "You haven't changed a bit," she said. And by that she meant he was still a lying, cheating scoundrel.

"You look more beautiful than the day we got hitched."

The cute redheaded waitress came over. "Hey, Woody. How's it hanging?"

He was clearly uncomfortable by the overly friendly remark. "I'm good. How about fetching us a couple of burgers and beers?"

"Iced tea, for me," Nina said.

The waitress shoved the pencil behind her ear, eyeing Nina suspiciously. "Sure thing."

After she left, Woody leaned back in his chair. "I hear you're calling yourself 'Nina' these days. Why the name change?"

"People grow up, you know. After Daddy dropped me from his will, I just didn't want to be called 'Edwina Granger' anymore."

He laughed. "Now that you just inherited his fortune, I guess that'll be different."

She sat up straight and tried not to glance down at the microphone. "And how exactly would you know that? Hmm? It wouldn't have something to do with that dowdy imposter you sent to impersonate me, would it?"

His grin was the same one that used to make Nina's insides turn to jelly. But now, all she wanted to do was slap the stupid look off his face. She clasped her hands in restraint.

"You know there ain't another woman in these parts that could take your place."

Nina folded her arms across her chest. "That's not an answer."

Woody squirmed under her stare. "Okay. You got me. I paid her to pretend to be you, but not for the reason you think. I did it for you."

She raised an eyebrow. "For me? How's that?"

"When I read in the paper that your brother killed himself, I figured you'd want possession of your daddy's estate. I figured I'd help the police come up with a motive to charge Allison, and the money and winery would all fall back in your lap. You're still my wife. I was doing you a favor. Who knew that your crazy papa would put that part in his will about suicide. Looks like you ended up with the money either way."

The waitress returned with their drinks and set them on the table with no comment.

Woody picked up his glass. "Here's to the richest woman in Maycroft."

Nina stared at him. "You thought you were doing me a favor?"

Woody took a drink. "That's right, baby. Now you and I can get back to runnin' the vineyard like we did before."

"Like when you and Drew were stealing from Daddy?"

"We won't have to do that now. It'll be all ours."

Nina took a sip of tea. She thought carefully about her next words. "It was pretty clever of you to make Daddy's will work in our favor."

Woody rubbed his chin. "What do ya mean?"

"You know. Making sure Drew was dead before his thirty-fifth birthday." Nina studied Woody's face. She wasn't sure if he was acting or if he was truly confused.

"You're gonna have to tell me what you're talking about, babe. I'm not sure I follow."

"Daddy's will said when he turned thirty-five, Drew could do whatever he wanted. But I guess you knew that already." She put her hand on his cheek and smiled. "Very smart of you."

"Sure. I guess so. Rita—that's the girl who pretended to be you—didn't say nothin' about that."

"But she didn't have to, right? You already knew when—you visited Drew that night."

Woody tilted his head and grinned. "Are you sure that iced tea ain't spiked or something? I don't know what you're talkin' about."

Nina was still unsure if Woody was playing her. He had always been a great conman. Like the time he told her he lost his wedding ring when he'd really pawned it to fly off to Vegas for the weekend. She pulled his head close to her mouth and whispered, "I know you shot my brother."

He jerked back. "What? You're talkin' crazy now. I never shot your brother. I was just takin' advantage of the situation. You don't think I'm a killer, do you?"

Nina pulled back. "It's okay, sugar. I'm not going to tell anyone. It's just you and me here. And now we're going to be rich. I just need to know the truth so that I can trust you."

Woody shook his head. "Is this because of that article in the newspaper that said someone may have murdered Drew? And you think it was me?"

Just then the waitress brought their food.

Nina pushed away her plate and folded her arms on the table. "Well, if not you, then who?"

It was Woody who leaned forward and whispered this time. "Maybe it was you."

Nina laughed. "Now, how would I have done that from way over in Nevada?"

"Then there's only one other person I can think of." Woody opened the ketchup bottle and dumped a big glob on his plate.

"And who would that be?"

"The only person who might have known about your daddy's will, of course. Your sister-in-law, Allison."

Chapter 22

DAN CARSON ACTUALLY smiled when Deena walked into his office later that afternoon. The buzz of the newsroom seemed a tad louder as computers hummed, printers clacked, and reporters scurried about.

Deena paused in the doorway. "What's going on? Did someone rob a bank or something? Did Mr. Crane's pet python escape again?"

Dan pushed the knot up tighter on his necktie. "*You* happened, that's what." He held up a stack of papers. "Look at all these letters to the editor that have come in. The whole town is up in arms over the mishandling of the Granger case, and it's all because of your story."

Suddenly, Deena's mouth felt like the Mojave Desert. She wasn't used to this kind of reaction to her work. She assumed most of her stories ended up lining Mrs. Potts's birdcage or as packing material for people moving. She plopped down in a chair.

"Am I in trouble again?"

"Heck no! You're about to be named Employee of the Month and you don't even work here yet. Oh, about that." He pulled a folder out of his bottom desk drawer. "Lloyd Pryor wants to get you under contract right away so we can change your byline from 'contributor' to 'staff writer.' Here's your contract." He held out the folder and a pen.

"Whoa down, hoss. Let me ask a few questions first." She took in a deep breath and let it out slowly. "We still don't know if Andrew was murdered, right?"

"That doesn't matter." He caught sight of the raised eyebrow Deena shot him. "I mean, of course it matters. It's just that the investigation was flawed. When it got out that Detective Guttman wasn't in town and didn't sign off on the investigation, rumors started flying. Apparently, others have speculated about Allison Granger's affair and possible involvement."

"But those are just rumors. We haven't seen any solid evidence."

"Exactly." Dan leaned back in his chair and clasped his hands behind his head. "That's where you come in. You've got to keep digging and make sure the police do their job."

It all sounded a bit underhanded to Deena. Obviously, she wanted justice for Drew, but was this the right way to go about it?

As though he had read her mind, Dan tried his best to allay any doubt she was feeling. "Look, Deena, if you want to be a journalist, this is what we do. It's the same as when you worked as an investigator for that defense attorney. The only difference is that we give the facts to the public." He paused. Then, "Remember when we solved the case of the woman strangled by her knitting? You were proud of our work then, weren't you?"

She nodded.

"You'll be proud of this story, too, when it's all said and done."

Dan had made a good point. Although, she was determined not to embellish the facts just to sell newspapers. Still, it felt like a lot of responsibility on her shoulders. "But what if it turns out that it was just a suicide? Then I will have stirred up a hornet's nest for nothing."

"Not for nothing. For the truth." He loosened his tie again. "I'll admit that a homicide would make a better story, but we can only go where the facts take us. Okay?" He held out the pen again.

"Okay. But I'm not ready to sign yet. I want to make sure you hold up your end of the bargain."

"I like your skepticism."

She took the pen from him. "This pen is going to be your word that we are only going to print the facts."

"Yes, ma'am."

"Oh, and speaking of facts, you better check your sources more carefully. According to Allison, she isn't pregnant."

"What?" Dan tossed the folder on the stack of files. "That's not what she's been telling people. I got that from two different women at the hair salon."

Deena laughed. "*You* go to the hair salon?" She pictured Dan with one of those vinyl leopard capes draped over his shoulders.

He set his jaw defensively. "How else do you think we get leads? It's not gossiping. It's networking."

She had a sudden sinking feeling and wondered if her own hairdresser had loose lips. "You don't happen to go to Kristy at the Manely Beauty Salon, do you?"

"No, Cheryl."

Cheryl worked at the station right next to Kristy. She was indeed a gossip. Relieved, Deena got out her notes and started catching Dan up with events from the reading of Drew's will and the meeting between Nina and Woody Davenport.

Dan was impressed. "You really used a hidden tape recorder? Way to go, cutie. But you know we can issue you one from here."

"I didn't think of that," she confessed. "Anyway, it turned out to be nothing. Woody was just playing another one of his cons."

"Still, you haven't ruled out the sister."

Deena shook her head. "Nina? She didn't kill her brother, I'm sure of it."

Dan steepled his fingers with his elbows resting on the desk. "Based on what? Your gut or facts?"

"Based on the fact that she was in Nevada when Drew died."

"Says who?"

Deena huffed and threw out her hands. Why was he being so obstinate?

Dan's face softened. "Look, I'm not trying to frustrate you, I'm just pointing out the facts. It's the job of the police to track down the killer, if there is one. We just raise the questions. Have you talked to Guttman since the story broke?"

"No. I have a feeling he doesn't want to talk to me."

Dan grinned. "Since when did that stop you?"

"Good point."

Dan stood and walked around the desk. "I want you to file your story about the estate going to Andrew Granger's sister. That's fact as well as public information. Then talk to Guttman and see if they are reopening the investigation. Call me later and fill me in."

Deena followed him to the door. "In the meantime, trust no one. Is that right?"

"You got it, cutie."

Chapter 23

THE NAGGING FEELING that she was making a murder out of a molehill made for a restless night's sleep for Deena. Maybe Drew had been suicidal and had taken his own life. The people who would know best were his wife and coworkers. She couldn't trust Allison to be honest, since it was in her best interest to claim someone murdered her husband. If it turned out to be true, she would get her husband's inheritance, including his life insurance. No, she needed to speak to people Drew had worked with.

Maybe his secretary would have an opinion about Drew's state of mind leading up to his death. After all, it's usually the secretary at any business who really keeps the place running. That was certainly true when Deena was a high school teacher. If you wanted to know anything about your supply order or the school calendar, you always bypassed the principal and went straight to the school secretary.

As Deena headed back to the winery Wednesday morning, she knew that Vera Clausen would be the first person on her list to question. Hopefully, she would be able to avoid Lonnie Fisher this time around. She had a feeling he wasn't happy with her stirring up trouble for the vineyard.

Vera was working a crossword puzzle and had her feet up on a space heater when Deena entered the office. She looked up as Deena stood in front of the desk.

"Oh dear. I didn't hear you come in. You're Mrs. Sharpe, right? Is Mr. Fisher expecting you? If so, he didn't tell me about it. No one tells me anything anymore. People just come and go as they please. Whether it's the police, or a buyer, or—"

"Did you say police?" Deena took the liberty of pulling one of the chairs in the waiting area up to Vera's desk.

Surprisingly, Vera reacted as if they were old friends having a chat. "Yes. That detective from the Maycroft PD was here yesterday. Asked me a bunch of questions about the business and the Grangers and such. He sure is handsome."

What was with these women? When he first arrived in Maycroft, Linus Guttman was like a city slicker at a rodeo. He grew a beard, and suddenly he was the belle of the ball. "Um, I guess. What sort of things did he tell you?"

Vera leaned in and lowered her voice. "I can trust you, can't I? I know you're the reporter writing those stories about Mr. Granger. I need this job, so I don't want my name in the paper."

Deena flashed her empty hands. "No notes, I promise. I'm just looking for background information."

Vera proceeded to tell Deena the most mundane, inconsequential facts about Granger's Grapes she could imagine. Everything from how the guys in the field kept stealing each other's lunches to who was using their company cell phone for personal business. She could only imagine how Detective Guttman would have reacted to such nonsense. But then the woman said something that caught her attention.

"Layla Baxter—she's the bookkeeper—acts like she's the boss around here. She's the only one allowed to go into Mr. Granger's office, besides Mr. Fisher, of course. Rumor has it she used her big raise last year to get a 'big raise' for her ta-tas, if you know what I mean."

Deena nodded. "Disgraceful. But you aren't suggesting she was sleeping with one of the bosses, are you?"

"Oh heavens, no. Neither of them seemed interested in her. They never seemed to socialize. Now, the guys working the field are a different matter."

"I see." Deena noticed Vera's calendar. It was almost blank except for some doodling. "Let's go back to the week Mr. Granger died. Did you notice anything unusual about his demeanor?"

Vera grinned. "That's the same question that detective asked me. Like I told him. Mr. Granger seemed more worried than usual. Not sad, but stressed. He and Mr. Fisher both seemed stressed. Neither said anything to me directly, but Mr. Fisher nearly took my head off when I asked him where he was going when he left early that day."

"What day?"

"The day Mr. Granger died."

"That seems suspicious. Did you tell Detective Guttman?"

Vera glanced over her shoulder in the direction of the hallway leading to Lonnie's office. "I did. He said he would be back to talk to Mr. Fisher."

"Why didn't he talk to him yesterday?"

"Mr. Fisher had gone up to Dallas on business and wasn't here."

Deena wanted to talk to the bookkeeper to see if she knew anything about why Drew was upset those days leading up to his death. But first, she had another idea. She wanted to know where Lonnie Fisher had gone that day. "Do you know if Mr. Granger kept a personal calendar?"

Vera nodded. "Oh sure. He wrote down everything."

"Is there a chance I could see it?"

"You'd have to ask Layla. She keeps Mr. Granger's door locked ever since..." She scratched her head. "That's right. You were the one who snuck into his office."

Deena felt her face redden. "Um, uh..."

"Don't worry. I understand that you are a reporter and were just doing your job." Then she leaned her generous bosom on the desk and whispered to Deena, "I suppose you want to know what was written on his calendar on the day he died."

Deena's eyes widened as she mouthed the word "yes."

"It said 'Allison's book club.'"

That was the big secret? It matched exactly what Allison had said.

Deena saw Vera look up with wide eyes before she heard the voice behind her.

"Mrs. Clausen! I'm not paying you to sit around here and gossip."

Deena spun around to face Lonnie. "We weren't gossiping. We're networking."

"Mrs. Sharpe," he said, in a less accusatory tone. "I didn't realize that was you."

She flashed her most innocent-looking smile. "I just came by to ask a few questions."

"I'm glad you did." Lonnie helped her up by the arm. "Let's go to my office so we can talk in private." He glared at Vera and then led Deena down the hall.

"Please have a seat." Lonnie was once again dressed impeccably, although his shoes had a little less shine and the knot on his tie was looser than before.

Deena pulled out her notepad in order to signal she was there on official newspaper business. "I understand that Detective Guttman was here yesterday asking questions."

He half rolled his eyes. "No doubt Vera got a kick out of telling you that. Apparently, she wanted to make a big deal over my whereabouts the day Drew died. As I will explain to Detective Guttman, I drove up to Dallas to check on a warehouse space we have made an offer on. I have a witness who can verify I was there. Would you like his name?"

Lonnie's demeanor was calm except for his aggravation with his secretary. "That won't be necessary. I'm really here to ask about Drew's mood and behavior on the days leading up to his death. I know you said he was unhappy with Allison, but I wondered if you thought he was depressed?"

Lonnie leaned back in his chair and folded his hands. He seemed to study Deena for a long moment. This time there was no ring on his finger, only an indentation where it once was. "You lied to me," he said at last.

"Pardon me?"

"The last time you were here you said you were writing a sort of tribute to Andrew. The article in the newspaper was hardly a tribute."

Deena held her head erect. "As it turns out, there was a new angle to the story as I started digging into the matter. It's not like I wrote anything derogatory about him."

"True enough." Lonnie pulled something out of his desk drawer. "In fact, I wasn't completely honest with you either." He passed her the piece of paper. "Here. Read this."

It was a piece of cream-colored linen stationery embossed with the letter *G*. She opened it up and read:

My beloved queen,

I hope you will find it in your heart to forgive me after all these years we have been together. I know the pain I have caused you and wish I could take it all away. I can't bear to be with you any longer under the circumstances. I wish I could. Even though we will no longer be together, I will always carry you in my heart.

Love always,

Drew

Deena read it again, her chest tightening with every word. "This sounds like a suicide note. Where did you get it?"

"I found it in Drew's drawer the day he died." He took out a handkerchief and wiped his forehead.

"Did you show it to anyone? Did you show it to Allison?"

As Lonnie stuffed the handkerchief back in his pocket, he shook his head. "No. I didn't have the heart to. I thought she had suffered enough without knowing she was the cause of her husband's suicide." He reached for the note and stared at it.

Deena mulled over the words she had just read. What did Drew mean by "under the circumstances"? She asked Lonnie if he knew.

"I can only speculate that he was talking about their marriage." He folded up the note and laid it back on his desk.

"Could it have something to do with Allison being pregnant?"

Lonnie jerked his head back and glared at Deena. "Mrs. Sharpe. That is the second time you have made that accusation. I believe Allison made it very clear the other day at her attorney's office that she is not pregnant."

Remembering what Dan had said, she shot back, "Then why was she going around telling everyone she was?"

"I guess you'd have to ask her that."

Deena stood up. "I plan to. And while I'm at it, I think Detective Guttman should see that suicide note. He'll want to verify its authenticity. After all, it could be the proof he needs to rule Drew's death a suicide."

Lonnie walked around his desk to stand by Deena. "Mrs. Sharpe, I didn't mean to antagonize you. I know you are just doing your job. We are all devastated by Drew's death. I should have come forward with this note before. It wasn't until yesterday that I realized the detective was taking another look at the case."

Deena looked into his wet eyes. The man's grief was obvious. "I'm sorry to have been so defensive, it's just that I'm the reason for this whole mix-up. I'm the girl who cried 'murder,' and I feel just awful about it."

Lonnie reached for the note and handed it to Deena. "Here. Take this to Allison or the police or whoever. I know you just want to see justice done. I was probably wrong for keeping it to myself. Do what you think is right."

Deena was surprised but relieved to have solid evidence. "Thank you, Lonnie. I think I should show it to Allison in person and give her a chance to come to grips with it before I give it to Detective Guttman."

"That sounds best to me, too." Lonnie reached out and shook her hand. "Good luck."

Although it was another tight squeeze, at least his ring didn't bore into her skin.

As she turned to leave, Lonnie added one last request. "If possible, Mrs. Sharpe, could you please keep Drew's last words out of the newspaper? I'm sure he meant them to stay private."

"I will." As she headed out to her car, she worried about Dan. Knowing him, he'd want to publish a photocopy of the note in the newspaper. She tucked the note safely in her handbag. It would be tricky, but she'd have to figure out a way to keep the note out of her editor's hands.

If Allison could verify that Drew indeed wrote the suicide note, it would be time to mark this case as closed.

Chapter 24

HOW COULD SHE HAVE let things get so far out of hand? Was she blinded by ambition? Perhaps her desire to make a name for herself clouded her good sense. Whatever it was, she was prepared to eat crow when Guttman ruled Drew's death a suicide...*again.*

Her first hurdle, however, would be showing Allison the letter. Not only would she probably feel responsible for her husband's death, but it would make it even harder for her to claim her rights to the Granger estate. Her attorney had a big fight on his hands if they were going to challenge Edward Granger's morals clause.

Deena's cell phone rang. It was an unknown number. She debated letting it go to voicemail, but her curiosity won out. "Hello?"

"Mrs. Sharpe, it's Allison Granger. I was hoping we could get together to talk."

"Are you at work?"

"No, I took the week off. I'm at home."

"Perfect," Deena said. "I'll be right over."

* * *

"WHAT A COINCIDENCE that you were wanting to see me when I called." Allison waved Deena into the den. "Do you want some coffee?"

"Sure, if you are having some."

"Are you kidding? I've been living on coffee for the past two weeks." She headed to the kitchen. "Cream and sugar?"

"Yes. Lots of both."

Pregnant women don't drink gallons of coffee, at least not these days. Deena glanced around the room. There were plenty of photographs of Allison and Drew. Most looked like vacation pictures. They appeared happy. The most obvious sign of disarray was the stack of bills and legal papers strewn across the dining table.

Allison returned with the coffee. The not-so-merry widow was looking drab in her jeans and oversized Dallas Cowboys jersey. Deena wondered if it had belonged to Drew. Judging from the pictures, it would probably have been big on him too.

"Excuse the mess," she said and handed a cup to Deena. "I'm up to my eyeballs in paperwork. Drew paid all the bills, and I'm trying to figure out what's what." She took a gulp from the steaming cup. "I used to think all he was good for was killing the occasional spider in the bathroom. Boy, was I wrong."

No tears spilled from her eyes, but she did have a quiet, melancholy sadness about her. It could have been the mountain of bills, or it could have been something else. Had the couple been facing financial trouble? If something ever happened to

Gary, Deena knew she'd be totally lost when it came to paying their bills and taking care of finances. Maybe Allison was just overwhelmed by it all.

"So why did you want to talk to me?" Allison stared over her cup as though it were a shield protecting her from the harsh questions she anticipated.

Deena glanced down at her handbag that housed the suicide note from Drew. "Why don't you go first. Tell me why you called me."

"Well, I wanted to see where you were on your murder investigation. Maybe there is something I can add to help find Drew's killer. He had some enemies, you know. Maybe one of them did it."

"Enemies? Like who?"

"Like his sister for one. And her husband, too, I guess. And what about that woman who was pretending to be his sister."

Remembering Dan's caution about who to trust, Deena debated defending Nina and Woody or letting Allison believe they were out to get their hands on her fortune. Now that she was certain Drew had killed himself, it didn't much matter. Still, she didn't want to make the relationship between Allison and Nina any worse. "From what I can tell, neither was involved in Drew's death, although Woody was hoping to cash in on the money. I don't think you should worry about them."

"Then how about Owen Walsh. He said some nasty things at the funeral. Drew never explained why there was bad blood between the two of them, but he had told me to keep away from him."

Deena started to explain about the stolen vines, when she was saved by the bell...literally.

"Who could that be?" Allison turned toward the front door. When the doorbell ring was followed by a knock, she got up to see who it was.

Deena took that moment to retrieve the note from her bag. No use putting it off any longer. She needed to tell Allison the truth.

When Allison opened the front door, Barbara Potts from next door stood there holding a plate covered in aluminum foil and proceeded to push her way into the house. "Well, hello again," she said to Deena. Then she turned back to Allison. "I didn't know you had company, dear."

Deena offered up a little wave. Of course, the woman knew Allison had company since Deena's car was parked right out front.

"I brought you over a little something to eat." Barbara pulled back the foil to reveal a plate of four cat hair-covered cinnamon rolls that looked ready for the garbage bin. She glanced around. "I see you're having coffee. These will go perfectly. Let me just pour myself a cup and I'll put these on some plates. This way to the kitchen, right?"

"None for me," Deena called out a bit too anxiously. She shot a frightened look at Allison and shook her head ever so slightly.

"Me either," Allison chimed in. "But thanks."

When Barbara was out of earshot, Deena whispered to Allison, "I have something I need to show you." She handed her the note and watched Allison's face as she read.

Her eyes began to tear up and she covered her mouth to stifle a cry. When she finished, she looked up at Deena. "Where did you get this?"

"Lonnie found it in Drew's office. Is that his handwriting?"

Allison looked back at the note and nodded. "So he did...kill himself."

Deena patted the grieving widow on the back. "It sure sounds that way."

Barbara came in and plopped down on the chair opposite the two women on the sofa. Allison shoved the note at Deena, who stuck it back in her handbag.

Not totally blind to her neighbor's grief, Barbara set the plate of furry pastry down on the coffee table. "Now, dear, you mustn't let this keep upsetting you. You're a pretty, young thing. How old are you? Forty? Forty-five? You'll find another man in no time."

Deena's jaw dropped. Not only was Allison in her early thirties, her husband wasn't even in the ground yet. So much for grief counseling.

Barbara continued. "I mean, I know you're lonely now, but that won't last long. Besides, you can do better than a man like Andrew Granger. Best thing about him was his money." Barbara sipped her coffee.

The tension rose in Allison's face. Deena put an arm across her stiffening shoulders and said, "Now, Barbara, that's not very kind."

"Kind? Allison knows what I'm talking about. Since he's been dead, she hasn't had to call the police over here even one time."

Allison gasped and put her hand to her chest.

"I know, dear," Barbara said. "You thought it was a secret. You even had them park down the street sometimes, but I saw.

You don't have to worry about him beating you or bullying you or Lord knows what, ever again."

Allison's face reddened and she looked like a balloon about to pop.

"Why don't you go in the bedroom and pull yourself together." Deena hoisted her off the sofa. "I'll explain things to Barbara for you." She practically pushed Allison down the hallway.

When Deena returned, Barbara had more to say. "Did I say something wrong? I was just pointing out how that nice Officer Linndorf hasn't come around even once since her husband shot himself. *If* he shot himself, that is. If I didn't know better, I'd say Allison did him in herself and just made it look like a suicide. Could you blame her? Men are the worst."

Just then a shrill scream came from the other side of the house. It was Allison. Had she seen a mouse? Stumbled across another dead body? Deena froze as she faced one of those fight or flight moments. Her first thought was to run. What if Allison was looking down the barrel of a gun held by an intruder? But then her mama-bear instinct kicked in and she ran toward the hallway and smack into Allison.

"What on earth is it?" Deena held the woman's arms and looked her over for stab wounds.

Allison, grinning like a Cheshire cat, held up her cell phone. "That was Eric Lyons. He found a loophole. I'm going to get the estate after all!" She did a little happy dance.

"Congratulations!" Barbara said, holding a half-eaten cinnamon roll in her hand.

Deena felt light-headed and her knees buckled. Luckily, Allison caught her and helped her to the sofa.

"Are you okay, dear?" Barbara asked. "Maybe you just need a bite to eat." She offered up a cinnamon roll.

Deena held up her hand in protest. "No. I'm fine." The truth was that between standing up too quickly and seeing the disgusting pastry in Barbara's mouth, she nearly lost her breakfast. She put her hand on her stomach to quiet it down.

"You gave me a scare," Allison said as she stood over Deena. "I thought you were going to faint."

"Me too," Barbara said as she licked icing from her fingers. She stuck out her tongue and scraped off a hair. "For a minute, I thought *you* were the one pregnant instead of Allison."

Allison spun around. "What? Listen here, both of you. I. Am. Not. Pregnant. And I'd appreciate if you'd both leave. Now."

Deena was halfway to the door when she heard Barbara send up one last parting blow to Allison. "You sure are acting high and mighty for someone who may have murdered her husband. You're going to wish you had friends like Mrs. Sharpe and me when the truth comes out."

Chapter 25

WELL, THAT DIDN'T GO as planned. Deena wasn't sure whether to drive to the police station to show the suicide note to Guttman or just go home and crawl under the covers with her dog, Hurley. She pulled into a gas station to fill up her car and think.

As she got out, a police car with lights flashing pulled in behind her. *If that's Officer Linndorf, I'm definitely going home.*

It wasn't. It was his former partner, Clay Hitchcock, the guy who had signed off on Linndorf's investigation of Drew's death.

"Mrs. Sharpe," he said and tipped his hat. "Didn't realize that was you."

She doubted that. Was she now being harassed by law enforcement? She had heard of cases where journalists were targeted for criticizing the police department, but she never dreamed it would happen to her.

"What is it, Officer Hitchcock? I wasn't speeding. Are you going to ticket me for going too slow?"

The policeman looked like a confused puppy. "What? No. You have a brake light out."

"Sure I do."

"No, really. Look." He opened her car door and put his foot inside to apply the brake.

She walked around to the rear of her car. Sure enough, the left light did not come on. This really wasn't her best day. "Sorry. I'll get it fixed as soon as possible."

"I wasn't going to write you a citation." He scribbled on a pad and then tore off the paper and handed it to her. "Here's a warning. You have twenty-four hours to get it fixed." He tipped his hat again and grumbled as he walked back to his car, "Have a nice day."

Deena looked at the police car and had a hunch. "Officer Hitchcock, were you ever called out to the Granger house over a domestic dispute?"

"No. Never."

"Are you sure?"

"Yes. Why?"

She pulled the gas hose off the cradle and stuck the nozzle in her tank. Then she walked up to the police car. "Do you know where I can find Officer Linndorf right now?"

"Right now, you should be heading to a mechanic to get that brake light fixed."

Deena rolled her eyes. "Come on. I just want to ask him a few questions."

"This is about Andrew Granger, am I right?"

"Right."

"Look, Mrs. Sharpe, I was there in the house after that guy shot himself. It wasn't a homicide. It was suicide. Textbook case." He pulled a toothpick out of parts unknown and stuck it in his mouth.

"Then what's the harm of asking a few questions?" She tried to bat her eyes, but it looked more like a nervous tick.

"Reporters. Sheesh." He rolled the toothpick with his tongue as he eyed her suspiciously. Finally, he gave up the stare-down. "He should be over on Pecan and Third."

She grinned. "The speed trap by the liquor store?"

"That's the place."

Deena thanked him and finished putting gas in her car as he drove away. While she stood next to the pump, she felt her strength return. *Textbook case, huh?* Once a teacher, always a teacher; and she was about to add a whole new chapter to that textbook. If her theory was right, this case was about to blow wide open.

* * *

WHEN SHE GOT TO THE intersection, she spotted Linndorf's police cruiser parked right next to the liquor store where she expected it to be. But the officer wasn't in it. She pulled in front of the store and went inside. A quick glance around told her Linndorf wasn't there. She asked the man behind the counter.

"Check out back," he said, motioning with his thumb toward the alley. "He's probably with those kids from the neighborhood."

Deena walked around to the rear of the store. As it turned out, those "kids" were teenagers who should have had better things to do than play ball in the middle of a school day.

Linndorf stood on a flattened cardboard box that served as a pitching mound. One of the boys had a catcher's mitt and punched it with his fist. "Come on, cop, put it here." He held up the glove.

Crouched over the catcher was another boy aiming a radar gun at Officer Linndorf, who checked the imaginary bases and then went into his windup. The ball sailed into the target, hitting the catcher's mitt with a loud smack.

"Wowzer!" the boy with the radar gun shouted. "That was your best one yet, cop. Seventy-two miles an hour."

Linndorf grinned as the catcher threw back the ball. Then he caught sight of Deena standing next to the building. "Scram, fellows. I'll catch up with you later." As the boys took off, Linndorf turned to Deena. He stuck out his chin defiantly. "Can I help you, Mrs. Sharpe?"

"Just wondering if you've seen anyone around here contributing to the delinquency of minors?"

"Very funny." He brushed past her, picked up the radar gun, and put it in his car. "What do you want? I've got work to do."

"I can see that." How else was he planning to waste the taxpayers' money? "I wanted to talk to you about the Granger case."

Linndorf folded his long legs and got in the car. "Talk to Guttman. It's out of my hands."

"Okay. I'll tell him you were the one having an affair with Allison Granger."

"What?" He got out and slammed the door. He hurried over and grabbed Deena's elbow, leading her back to the alley. "Who told you that?"

"You did just now by your reaction."

His eyes grew dark and his brows sank deep over his lids. "It's not true."

"Yes it is. That's why the neighbor kept seeing your car over there all the time. Was it for twilight rendezvous or afternoon delights?"

"Who told you? Allison?"

"Let's just say a little bird told me. And what a coincidence that you were the first officer on the scene when Drew was shot." As soon as the words came out of her mouth, she felt another sinking feeling. Could Linndorf have something to do with Drew's death? No. It was a suicide. She had the proof in her purse.

But why was she confronting him in a blind alley on the wrong side of town? She needed to get out of there. With no real plan, she turned and started hurrying toward the side of the building.

"Wait!" Linndorf grabbed her arm. His hand went to his gun. He rested it there. "I need to think."

His grip on her arm was strong. She wanted to scream but felt her throat tighten. It was like one of her nightmares where she would try to yell for help, but no words would come out. Then she pulled her arm and he let her go.

He was breathing heavy now. "If you say anything, I'll lose my job." He began to pace. "What have I done? What have I done?"

Deena wanted to tell him that he got tangled up in a homicide investigation and hadn't been honest about his relationship with the victim's wife. Instead, she made a dash for safety.

"Wait!" he yelled again. "I'm coming, too."

What? Standing next to her car, she dug in her purse for the keys. What was he saying?

"Let me tell Guttman first. Maybe he'll go easier on me." Linndorf got in his car and sped off.

Deena found her keys and stood there for a moment in disbelief. Was he really going to the station to confess to hanky panky, or was this just a really weird dream?

Chapter 26

DEENA STOOD AT THE counter inside the police station and asked to speak to Detective Guttman. She remembered the pretty female officer from her last visit on another case. Now that Deena was a crime reporter, she assumed they might be getting to know each other well.

The woman picked up the phone and made a call. Holding the receiver slightly away from her ear, she nodded and hung up. She leaned toward the opening in the glass partition. "Detective Guttman said he's in a meeting and wasn't to be disturbed."

"He'll want to talk to me, trust me."

The phone rang again. The woman said, "Yes, sir," and buzzed Deena through. She led Deena to Guttman's office, then said, "I don't know what you did, ma'am, but I sure wish you luck in there."

When Deena went inside, Officer Linndorf was leaning against the wall with his hat in his hand. He looked smaller than he had in the alley. He kept his eyes lowered.

Guttman grunted a greeting and motioned for Deena to sit. "Off the record. Understand?" He glared across his desk at her.

"Hmm. I'm not so sure I can agree to that." She stroked her chin with an exaggerated flourish as she contemplated the request.

Guttman was in no mood for games. "Either that, or get out."

"Off the record."

Guttman sat back in his chair authoritatively. "It's my understanding that you know something about the Granger case that has just come to light. I want us to get everything out in the open so there are no more allegations of mishandling of the case. Is that clear?"

"Yes, sir," Deena and Linndorf said in unison.

Guttman slapped a file folder on his desk. "Officer Linndorf has stated that he was having an affair with Mrs. Granger at the time of Mr. Granger's death. Obviously, we frown on our officers consorting and such, but that's beside the point."

"Is it?" Deena picked up her handbag and set it in her lap. "It would seem to be very much the point."

Guttman puffed out his chest as though he were the Big Bad Wolf about to blow her house down. "What I mean is that the more serious matter involves Officer Linndorf's investigation of the scene. He should have recused himself and let another officer take the lead. That's policy." He turned to Linndorf and addressed him like a drill sergeant. "State the policy number, Officer Linndorf!"

Larry scratched his head. "Uh...number three-something?"

Guttman's face reddened. "How could you have already forgotten? I just read it to you out of the handbook!"

Larry looked down at his feet again. "Sorry, sir. I guess I'm a little worn out. It's been a bad day."

Guttman was about to blow. "A bad day? Are you kidding me? What do you have to say for yourself?"

"I made a mistake. It's just that she was so pretty and every time I went to the bank to cash a check, she would flirt with me. You know how it is with us guys. What was I supposed to do?"

Guttman, exasperated, slapped his hand on his forehead.

Deena turned to Linndorf. "You know what the real problem is here, don't you?"

He fumbled with his hat. "No, what?"

"Direct deposit. You should never have to go to the bank these days unless you need to take out a loan. Even that can probably be done online."

Guttman rolled his eyes.

"I'm serious," she said with a wicked grin. "My husband does all our finances on the computer. He could show you how."

"Mrs. Sharpe!" Guttman roared. "You're not helping." He heaved a sigh. "Linndorf, go to your office and stay there until I call you. Do some paperwork. I'll deal with you later."

Linndorf put his hat back on his head, opened the door, and looked back at Deena. "You're a real smart lady. You should have been a cop."

"Thanks," Deena said awkwardly. She felt a little sorry for the guy since he was probably about to be fired. Hopefully, Ian wouldn't end up hiring him to replace her as an investigator.

As the officer stood there, he shook his head. "You know, I can see how you found out that I was having an affair with Allison, but what I can't figure out is how you knew I staged the crime scene to look like a suicide." With that, he walked out and closed the door behind him.

* * *

FOR A MOMENT, GUTTMAN and Deena just stared at each other. Then Guttman stood up and yelled, "*Linndorf!* Get back in here!"

The officer returned looking more hopeless than before. He held out his hands. "What did I do now?"

"Explain yourself."

Linndorf shifted his weight from one foot to the other. "Like I said. I thought Allison was cute. She had a smokin' hot body—"

"Not that!" Guttman looked as though the veins on his head would burst any minute. "What do you mean you staged the crime scene to look like a suicide?"

"I thought I told you," he said. Then to Deena, "I thought *she* told you."

Deena pressed her lips together and stared wide-eyed. She was afraid if she said the wrong thing, Guttman might have a coronary right there at his desk. She wondered where they kept the defibrillator just in case.

Guttman plopped back in his chair, loosening his tie and unbuttoning his top shirt button the way Dan did the other day.

"Let's all just sit down and figure this out." Guttman forced a smile and waved his arm for Linndorf to sit in the chair next to Deena.

"Thanks," Linndorf said. "My feet were killing me."

"Are you comfortable now?" Guttman asked with exaggerated sarcasm. "Can I get you anything to drink? Something to eat?"

Linndorf didn't get it. "Actually, I could use—"

"Shut up! I have a mind to call the DA right now and have him lock you up and throw away the key."

A stare-down between the two men ensued, with neither seeming to budge. Deena decided to give it a try. "Officer Linndorf—Larry—why don't you tell us exactly what happened that night you found Drew dead."

He turned to her and nodded. "I got the call, recognized the address, and headed right over. When I went in, the victim was laying on the bed with what looked like a gunshot wound to the head. Nothing was out of place, so I could tell it hadn't been a robbery. I saw the gun in a chair in the corner of the room. I panicked." He looked down at his hands.

"Why?" Deena asked. "What did you do next?"

"I closed the blinds so no one could see me—the bedroom was on the side of the house. I didn't want that lady next door and her husband to see what I was doing. I wiped down the gun with a bathroom towel, then pressed it in the victim's hand to get his fingerprints. Then I laid it next to him on the bed. I learned during my police training that some people do that. It worked perfectly, all right."

Guttman took notes the whole time even though he had turned on a small tape recorder. It was probably his way of keeping his emotions under control. Without looking up he asked, "And how long was it until Hitchcock arrived?"

"Four, maybe five minutes."

"What did you tell Hitch? Was he in on this with you?"

Linndorf sat up straight. "No, sir. He didn't know anything about it."

Guttman glared at him. "And now for the sixty-five thousand dollar question. Why?"

Linndorf squinted his eyes. "You mean, why didn't I tell Hitch what I did?"

"No," Deena said, intervening before Guttman went ballistic. "Why did you stage the scene to look like a suicide? Were you trying to protect someone?"

"You bet I was."

After a pause, she asked, "Who?"

"Myself, that's who. It was my fault he was dead. I never should have let it get that far. I'll know better next time, that's for sure."

Deena felt her last nerve start to catch fire. "Larry, who did you think shot and killed Andrew Granger?"

"Oh, I thought you'd figured it out. Allison, of course. I didn't want her to go to prison and drag me down with her. She wanted me to marry her. Told me she was pregnant. The last thing I wanted was to end up married to a jailbird and have to raise a kid. I know it was wrong, but now that you know, I guess you should go ahead and arrest her." He looked up at the detective.

"Um, just one problem with that, Einstein. *You destroyed the evidence!*" This time Guttman actually came out of his chair as he yelled.

"But it was obvious. It was Andrew's gun and it was in her house. She shot him right before she headed to the motel to meet me for...well, you know."

Guttman looked at Deena, his eyes pleading for someone with a little common sense to intervene.

She turned back to Linndorf. "Larry, you wiped the fingerprints off the gun. Now you can't prove who they belong to. Unless she confesses, you have no case."

"She didn't have to confess. I told her after the funeral that I couldn't see her again. It was pretty obvious she knew what she'd done. She said, 'So it was for nothing.' I said, 'That's right.' Then I left."

Guttman rubbed his forehead with his hand, and spoke slowly through gritted teeth. "Look, Linndorf, I want you to go lock yourself in the holding cage until I figure out what to do with you. Give your keys to the guard."

Linndorf gave him a hang-dog look and started toward the door.

"Give me your gun first." Guttman held out his hand.

Linndorf did as directed and closed the door behind him as he left.

"Do you really think he'll do it?" Deena asked.

"Of course. He's the dumbest officer on the force."

"So, what now?" She empathized with the position Guttman had found himself in.

"I need a favor. I need you to give me twenty-four hours before you put anything in the paper. I know it's a big story, but I need this. I'll owe you."

Deena shifted in her chair. "Do you really think Allison killed her husband?"

"I don't know. But what I do know is that I've got a lot of people to talk to. It's going to take hard work to prove a circumstantial case toward whoever committed this crime. The one thing I have working in my favor is the element of surprise. If you publish the news that it was definitely a homicide, I lose that."

"I understand. I'll wait until tomorrow, but that's it. I don't want it to look like I was involved in a cover-up." Deena stood up. "But where on earth are you going to start?"

Guttman opened the folder and pulled out a piece of paper. "Looks like I'm going to have to talk to that crazy cat lady."

Chapter 27

IT DIDN'T SEEM FAIR that Deena got to have all the fun, Gary thought as he changed from his suit to his work clothes. She got to flitter around town chasing criminals while he was stuck behind his desk in an office all day. This thought had driven him to leave work at lunchtime for a rare afternoon off.

He walked out the back door and sucked in a deep breath of cool Texas air. This was more like it. Deena didn't think he was serious about getting his hands dirty and working in the soil. The idea of running a vineyard had taken hold in his brain and wouldn't leave. He'd start with their backyard and prove how serious he really was.

Admittedly, he hadn't been tending to the landscaping lately, but it had been football season. His weekends were busy. The colorful pots where they'd planted tropical hibiscus plants and climbing Mandevilla were now homes to bare sticks. He went to the garage to find some work gloves. No use messing up his nails. Deena had just buffed them for him. He pushed around a bottle of antifreeze and another of bug spray to find the gardening supplies. Unlike his regular tools that hung neatly in rows on a pegboard wall, Deena kept her gardening paraphernalia in an old bucket.

Gary was quite proud of his garage and its organization. The tools looked pristine. If Deena needed a picture hung or a drawer handle tightened, he could go straight to the garage and find the right tool for the job. If his car needed servicing, he took it to Henry's Automotive. For cleaning, Doug's Detailing. And if a job around the house required a professional, Russell was just a phone call away.

He found the bucket and the gloves, checking them for spiders or other crawly critters before putting them on. He made quick work of the dead plants, putting them in large plastic garbage bags, and then carried the bags out to the curb for trash pick-up.

The swimming pool was another matter. He paid a service to come out regularly to check the water, keeping the chemicals balanced and the equipment functioning properly. But Gary had chosen to take care of the cleaning himself, which essentially meant sweeping out the leaves and emptying the skimmers once or twice a week. However, he'd gotten behind, being that it had been football season and all.

He pulled back the lid on the first skimmer basket timidly, knowing that the occasional field mouse or frog could have drowned and gotten swept up in there. He picked up the basket. Just leaves. After emptying it into the garbage, he repeated the task with the second basket.

Next, he pulled the long pole with a net on the end off the wall and began fishing out the floating debris. Thinking about how pleased Deena would be for his taking the initiative to tidy up the backyard, he walked over to a garbage bag to empty the net. When he turned it over, not one, but two small grass snakes wriggled out of the net and onto the patio.

If there was one thing Gary Sharpe was afraid of, it was snakes. It didn't matter that they were no bigger than your average earthworm, to him they were the same as rattlers and were out to sink their venomous fangs into his meaty flesh. He threw down the metal pole and ran around the house to the safety of the garage, where he stood in the corner trying to catch his breath.

He had to make a plan. What would happen if Deena came home and found him cowering in the garage? If he waited long enough, they might crawl away. But then they'd be in the grass. Hiding. Waiting.

A shovel was the answer. He went over to the storage bin that held all of his yard tools and picked up the shovel. When he did, he spotted a wasp nest in the corner of the ceiling. Shovel in hand, he reached up to knock down the nest, and out came a swarm of angry insects. He was outnumbered. Before he could get away, one got him on the hand. That's when he threw down the shovel, closed the garage door, and went inside to put ice on his throbbing hand.

And that's how Deena found him when she got home from the police station. He was sitting in his recliner, nursing his sore hand, watching basketball on TV.

* * *

HURLEY BARKED AS DEENA came through the door, which only intensified her anxiety. She couldn't imagine why Gary was already home from work unless he'd gotten sick or something had happened to a family member.

She gave Hurley a scratch on the top of the head to calm him down and rushed straight to the den. When she saw Gary in his recliner with an ice pack on his hand, she breathed a sigh of relief. "Good. You're okay." She took off her jacket and set down her purse. "What happened? Did you and the copy machine get into another fight?"

"Not exactly." He held up his hand. "I got stung by a wasp."

"A wasp? At the office?"

"No. In the garage."

She walked over to examine his hand. Without her reading glasses, she couldn't even make out where the sting had occurred. "I don't understand. Weren't you at work?"

Gary placed the ice bag back on his wound. "I took off early to work in the backyard. I thought you'd be happy."

She glanced out the French doors leading to the patio and spied the garbage bag. "I am, but I'm sorry about your hand." She plopped down wearily on the sofa. "While you were out playing in the yard, you'll never guess what happened."

Deena gave him the whole rundown. She told him about the suicide note Lonnie had found, her talk with Allison, and Detective Linndorf's confession to Guttman.

"Wow." Gary shook his head. "Sounds like you had a productive day."

Deena noted the lack of enthusiasm in his voice. "Okay, what's wrong now?"

He got up from the chair and walked over to the patio doors. "Nothing. While you tracked down leads, I pulled up weeds. That's all."

Deena sat back and crossed her legs. "Is this about the vineyard again?"

He nodded without turning around.

"Look," she said, "I've been thinking. You've been supportive about all my career moves, and I want to be supportive about yours. If you want to start a new business or get a new job or whatever, I'm fine with that. Just make sure it's something you really want to do. Trust me, it's no fun starting over every six months."

He spun around. "Good, because I've already started working on a business plan. I haven't worked out all the numbers yet, but I think it's doable. I'm sure I can get the financing, although I might want to consider taking on a partner. Someone who already knows the business."

And just like that, the conversation turned from murder to money. By the time they had finished dinner, they already had a list of possible names for their new winery.

Deena picked up her purse to take it to the bedroom when she spotted the note from Drew. She hadn't bothered to show it to Detective Guttman.

Gary walked by and saw her reading. "What is it? A love letter from Dan?"

"Of course not. Why would you say that?"

"Because he has a crush on you."

Deena made a sour face. "No, he doesn't."

"Sure he does," Gary said. "That's why he calls you cutie."

Deena followed Gary into the bedroom. "He calls me 'cutie' because he's sexist and he likens himself to the old beat reporters from the fifties. I'm surprised he doesn't wear one of those Jimmy Olsen hats."

"And because he likes you." Gary snatched the note out of Deena's hand. "So, what is it?"

Setting her handbag on the dresser, she pulled off her ear-rings. "It's Drew's suicide note."

"But you said he was shot by someone else." Gary read the note.

"I know. I wonder if he was thinking of killing himself, but someone beat him to it."

Gary handed it back to her. "I think you need to read this again. It's not a suicide note. It's a 'Dear John' letter—or 'Dear Jane' letter, in this case."

"What?" She pulled out her reading glasses to give it a good look.

He chuckled. "Hey, I know a breakup letter when I see one. I got several of them before I met you." He leaned in to kiss her cheek, but she pushed him away.

"Oh my gosh! I think you're right." She felt the hair on her arms stand up. "Drew wasn't about to kill himself, he was leaving his wife." She looked back at Gary wide-eyed. "You know what this is, right?"

Gary nodded. "A breakup note. Like I said."

"Yes, but it's also a motive. This could be the reason Allison shot her husband!"

She grabbed her keys. "I need to show this to Guttman." But just then, her cell phone rang. "It's Dan," she told Gary. "I should take this."

As usual, Dan skipped the pleasantries. "You need to get down to the jail. There's been a new development in your story. It just came over the police scanner that Allison Granger has been arrested."

Chapter 28

DEENA KNEW SHE DIDN'T have to rush. The booking process at the jail would take some time. Hopefully, she'd be allowed to see Allison or at least speak to her attorney.

Going to the jail had always been a depressing experience for Deena. The place was almost as cheerless as the emergency room at the hospital. Both had sad-colored walls and worry-worn carpet. The only real difference was that the lighting was a little brighter at the hospital.

As she sat in the waiting area, Deena wondered what new evidence the police had uncovered that had led to Allison's arrest. Did they really have enough to bring a murder case against her? How would this affect Drew's estate? Surely Allison wouldn't end up with it after this. Eric Lyons would have to find a loophole the size of Texas to be able to swing that.

Speaking of Eric Lyons, Deena wondered if he would be representing Allison in this matter. He generally handled family law and civil cases. It would be interesting to see if he would pass her off to someone else in his firm, especially since she probably was no longer worth a lot of money.

As though Deena had called forth his spirit, Lyons himself came walking out from the administration area of the jail.

"Mrs. Sharpe," he said as he spotted her. "Can't say I'm surprised to see you here."

"Are you representing Allison Granger in her murder case?"

"She wasn't arrested for murder. She's been charged with making false statements to the police. That's on the record, by the way."

For a minute, Deena had forgotten about the story. She was used to working with Ian Davis to defend indigent clients. "Really?" She took out a pad and pen. "Do you think they are just trying to find some reason to hold her until they get evidence to charge her with murder?"

"No comment."

Deena shifted to her reporter persona. "How does she plan to plead to the current charge?"

Lyons swapped his briefcase to the other hand. He must have come from home because he was wearing jeans and a polo shirt. "Not guilty, of course."

"Are you going to represent her yourself in this matter?"

Lyons blinked, obviously uncomfortable with the question. "I'll let you know after the hearing tomorrow. A lot will depend on Mrs. Granger's desires."

Like her desire to cheat on her husband with Larry Linndorf? Luckily, Deena hadn't said it out loud.

She jotted a note, then asked, "Can I see her?"

Lyons's eyebrows shot up as if to say, *You're kidding, right?* He took a step toward the exit. "You mean for a statement? We haven't had time to discuss it yet."

"But you wouldn't object, would you?" Deena knew she was walking a fine line. Her husband was an upstanding member of the community. She was a former teacher who had seen a number of the Lyons clan pass through her classes. But as a member of the press, she and the attorney were natural enemies.

Lyons was probably thinking the same thing as he measured the words of his response. "It is never in the best interest of a client to speak openly to the media without representation of an attorney, as I'm sure you know. Tomorrow, I will speak to my client about making a statement. She is anxious to clear up this matter, and inasmuch as the media can help in that regard, I'm sure she would appreciate cooperating in whatever manner is in her best interest."

Deena took that to mean "no."

As Lyons headed out the door into the evening dusk, she headed up to the window to request a visit with Allison Granger.

* * *

"YOU HAVE TEN MINUTES until visiting hours are over," the guard announced as Deena sat across from Allison and watched her through the plexiglass window. They each held a receiver in their hand and nodded their acknowledgement of the time restraint before the guard stepped away.

"I'm glad you came," Allison said.

Deena held up her hand. "Before you say anything else, is our discussion on the record for the newspaper?"

She shook her head. "No. My attorney told me not to speak to the press."

Deena wondered if she was wasting her time being there. "Then why did you agree to see me?"

"I have a question about the note you showed me this morning."

Deena couldn't believe their conversation had occurred that same morning. A lot had happened that day. Then suddenly Deena felt uncomfortable, realizing she could be holding a key piece of evidence in Drew's murder and had already shown it to the primary suspect. She tried not to glance down at her handbag. "What about it?"

Allison's expression took on a darker tone. "Why didn't you turn it over to Detective Guttman?"

It was a fair question. Should she give Allison the truth and say she forgot about it after snitching on her cop/boyfriend? She decided to use a tactic she'd learned from Guttman and asked a question instead. "Why? Why would it matter?" She fully expected for Allison to respond that it proved her husband had committed suicide.

But Allison tossed her another surprise. "Because I don't think it's a suicide note."

Deena took a few seconds to gather her thoughts. Where was Allison going with this? She pulled the letter from her bag. It wasn't like the other woman could reach through the plastic partition and take it from her. "What do you mean?"

"For one," Allison said, "I don't think it was addressed to me. If you look at it, Drew wrote, 'My Dearest Queen.' He never called me his queen. He always referred to me as his princess. And for another, I think he was talking about breaking up with whoever this *other woman* was."

There was disdain in her voice as she spoke about Drew's possible affair. Deena decided not to point out the obvious "pot calling the kettle black" situation. "Can you *prove* that he only called you 'princess'?"

"Sure. I have birthday cards and anniversary cards he wrote me over the years." She leaned in further. "But that's not my question. Why didn't you give the note to Detective Guttman? When he questioned me, I told him about it and that you had it, and he acted like I was crazy or lying or something. I need that note as part of my defense."

"I'll give it to him first thing in the morning. I promise." Deena checked her watch. "For the record, did you kill your husband?"

"No!"

"Then who do you think did?"

"Maybe the woman he was seeing behind my back."

"Any ideas who it could be?"

Allison shook her head. "That's what I've been trying to figure out all afternoon. When he wasn't home, he was at the winery. I was always suspicious about the bookkeeper there. Her name is Layla Baxter. Drew said he wasn't interested, but he could have been lying to me."

"Like you lied about going to book club every time you were going to meet Larry?" This time Deena had spoken her thoughts out loud.

"Okay. So, I lied to cover up my affair. Everyone does that."

"But you lied to the police, too."

"Technically, I didn't. Larry was at the house when I got there that night. Although he said he interviewed me about where I was and what I was doing, we actually never talked about it. I didn't know until today when Detective Guttman hauled me in that the suicide was staged. Larry broke up with me at the funeral and we haven't spoken since. For all I know, Larry may have killed Drew." Her eyes glistened with tears.

"It doesn't make sense that he would kill your husband and then dump you."

"I know. It's just that he was so angry with me."

"Angry about what?"

"Because I lied to him, too."

"About going to book club?"

The officer motioned that they only had three more minutes to talk.

Clearly Allison was getting frustrated with Deena. "Will you forget about the book club? Do I look like someone who reads? Even Drew probably knew that was a lie just so I could get out of the house."

Deena wasn't sure how to respond. Did readers really look any different from non-readers? She let it go. "So, what was the lie you told Larry?"

Allison let out a deep breath before answering. "I told both Larry and Drew that I was pregnant. I told them both that it was their baby."

At last, Allison had come clean about the pregnancy rumor. "Why did you do that?"

"I wanted to see which one would step up to the plate. Obviously, it wasn't Larry. He told me he was planning to break up with me that same night that he got the call about a gunshot at my house." She glanced up at the guard who gave her the "wrap it up" signal. She spoke faster now. "Ironically, Drew seemed okay about it, after he had a day to let it sink in. I think he was shocked since we hadn't been that...close lately. He promised to be a better husband and said he was happy. That was a few days before he died. I thought he may have changed his mind and killed himself. I felt so guilty. That's why I was happy when you said he might have been murdered."

"Time's up, ladies," the guard announced. "Visiting hours are over."

Just like the hospital, Deena thought.

Before she hung up the receiver, Allison made one final plea. "I need your help. Check out Layla Baxter. Talk to Detective—"

The guard pulled the receiver from Allison's hand and led her away.

Deena sat in stunned silence. Not only was she now unsure of Allison's guilt, she had now been asked to help defend her. She wasn't sure who she should call first—Dan or Detective Guttman.

She called Guttman.

That was a mistake.

Chapter 29

SHE COULD NOT STOP the one big tear from slipping down her face and splashing onto the keyboard as she wrote her story for the next day's edition. Dan had really let her have it for calling Guttman before him. She told him about everything she had done that day and which of the pieces of information were on the record and which were off.

He seemed moderately pleased with her progress and with the initiative she had taken in dealing with Linndorf, but when she told him she had promised to give Drew's note to Guttman, he went bonkers. That's when he launched into a ten-minute diatribe on the objectivity of the press. She was thinking too much like a defense investigator and not enough like a reporter. Her job wasn't to help Guttman or Allison or anyone. She was supposed to be digging out the facts and relaying them to the citizens of Maycroft via the newspaper.

Deena knew he was right. It was everything she learned in college and what she had taught her journalism students. After all, everyone in the case had their own agenda, even law enforcement. That's why sometimes they made a rush to judgment and accused the wrong suspect. Dan made it clear that if she was going to end up with a contract to work for the

Tribune, she had to pick whose side she was going to be on: the public's, the police's, or the accused's. He even implied he might have to put another reporter on the case.

She typed up her story, including the few new facts that she had gotten on the record. It wasn't much. Basically, all she could write was what she'd gotten from Eric Lyons. Everything about Linndorf was confidential for now. She imagined what the story would be if she could include everything she knew about the case. It would shed a lot of light on the investigation and especially the misconduct by the Maycroft Police Department.

Gary had left her alone when she first got home. After she proofed and emailed her story to Dan, she headed off to join him in the bedroom.

Gary was engrossed in a Harlan Coben mystery when she got in bed. He dog-eared the page and turned to look at Deena. "Why the red eyes? Are you tired or are your allergies kicking in?"

She tried to remain calm. "I talked to Dan. He's angry about the way I'm conducting the investigation."

"Angry? But you've made significant progress. If it weren't for you, the case would still be considered a suicide and a murderer would be on the loose with no one looking for him...or her."

"He said I care too much."

Gary's jaw dropped, but Deena continued before he came unglued. "He says I am too much on the side of the police and of Allison. And he's right. When I worked with Ian, it was easy to keep my eye on the ball. We would have a client we believed was innocent—or not getting a fair shake—and my job was to help find the truth in order to get justice."

Gary propped himself up on his pillow. "I don't see how that is any different than what you are doing now."

"But it is," she said. "I'm still trying to 'help' everyone, instead of being an objective outsider. Does that make sense?"

Gary shook his head. "Not really. Give me an example of something you would have done differently if you'd been playing by Dan's rules."

Deena waved her hand. "They're not just Dan's rules. But anyway, I would have published the note I'd gotten from Lonnie and let the chips fall where they may. At the very least, I would have used it as a bargaining chip to get Guttman to go on the record about Linndorf."

Gary digested her comment. He was beginning to see her point. "So, it's not the 'end' that would be different, it's the 'means.' Is that right?"

"Exactly," she said, offering up a faint smile. "I couldn't have stated it better myself. Which means that while I was running around playing junior detective, I wasn't doing my duty to the public. It's not that what I did was wrong, I just wasn't keeping the readers informed. As journalists, it is up to us to seek the truth and stay impartial."

Gary leaned over and put his book on the night table, then turned back to Deena. "Then that begs the question: Do you want to be an investigator or a reporter?"

"I was afraid you were going to ask me that." She reached up and turned off the bedside lamp. "I'll let you know when this case is over."

Chapter 30

GUTTMAN WAS READY TO deal. He knew good and well they could not make much of a case for murder against Allison Granger; and in fact, he confided to Deena that he wasn't even sure Allison was guilty. So when Deena came to the station the next morning offering to give him a new lead in exchange for information for her story, he jumped at the opportunity.

"You better have something good if you want me to go on the record about Linndorf and his affair with our chief suspect. That tidbit of news along with the staged suicide will send the townsfolk of Maycroft reeling." He gulped down the last of his coffee and folded the newspaper.

Deena sat next to him at the same coffee shop where she had first chatted with Nina Davenport the previous week. It seemed as though a lot had happened, although she was no closer to finding Drew's killer. At least she had Guttman on her side now. She was determined to solve the case and impress Dan Carson in the process.

"I spoke to Allison Granger last night at the jail." She sprinkled a third or fourth packet of artificial sweetener into her cup and stirred mindlessly.

"You what? I can't believe her attorney allowed it. Once she cried 'lawyer,' he wouldn't let her say another word to us."

Deena smiled, knowing she'd gotten one up on the detective. "She asked for my help."

"Does this have anything to do with that alleged suicide note she asked me about?"

"Yes and no."

Guttman scowled. "I'm in no mood for your little games."

"It's not a game. You see, we did talk about the note, but it turned out not to be a suicide note. Drew wrote it to break up with someone." Deena pulled it from her handbag. "Here."

After a quick read, he looked up. "Did Andrew Granger write this?"

"According to Allison, he did. However, she's not the person he wrote it to. She says he always referred to her as his 'princess.' If we can find out who this queen is, we may have another suspect with a motive."

Guttman turned the note over and looked at the back. "Where did you get this? From Allison?"

"No. Lonnie Fisher, Andrew's number two man at the vineyard, said he found it in Andrew's desk."

"So, you think the murder could have been committed by a jealous lover?"

"It's possible." Deena took a sip of coffee and spit it back into the cup. It was much too sweet. She pushed the cup away and wrung her hands nervously. "What do you think?"

"I guess it's as good a place to start as any. Do you have a nominee for Miss Killer Girlfriend?"

"Just one, actually. Allison said she was always suspicious of her husband's bookkeeper."

Guttman's eyebrows shot up. "I thought your husband was his bookkeeper. Are you saying Andrew Granger was gay?"

"No! Gary was his financial consultant. Big difference. A woman named Layla Baxter is the bookkeeper at Granger's Grapes. Apparently, she's a hot number."

"Well what are we waiting for? Let's go interview this hottie." He threw some bills on the table and stood up.

Deena pulled him back down to his seat. "Hold on, detective. It's a long way out there. Let's call and make sure she's there first."

"Hmm," Guttman said as he smoothed his hand across the back of his head. "We don't want to tip her off. I think a surprise visit would be best."

"I have an idea," Deena said. "I can call the receptionist and make sure Layla is there. Vera and I are like this." She held up her hand and crossed her fingers.

"Okay, but don't give her any details. We don't want this Baxter woman to sneak off or anything."

Deena nodded and dialed her cell phone. She recognized Vera's voice.

"Granger's Grapes. Could you please hold?"

Before Deena could respond, she was listening to some Frank Sinatra cover artist crooning "Fly Me to the Moon." She started to join in on the second chorus when Vera came back on the line.

"Thank you for holding. May I help you?"

"Vera, it's Deena Sharpe."

"Oh, hello, Mrs. Sharpe. I'm sorry for the wait. Things are nuts around here today, as you probably know."

"Why? What's going on?"

"There are several accountants here trying to audit the books and asking a whole bunch of questions I can't answer. Distributors are calling with questions...I'm drowning here."

"Surely Layla can handle them, right?" Deena winked at Guttman.

"Haven't you heard? She quit a few days ago. Luckily your husband agreed to drive out here to help. Is that why you called?"

"Um, yes. Sure." Deena turned away from Guttman.

"I'll put you through to him," Vera said.

When Gary got on the line, Deena asked him what was going on.

"Lyons sent over a few CPAs. It has to do with probating the will. Lonnie's not here and I'm really swamped. Do you need something important?"

"Just one thing. Do you know what happened to Layla Baxter?"

"According to Vera, she took a job at Never Too Fit."

"The new gym? Is she taking care of their books or what?"

"That's all I know, hon. I really need to go. See you at supper."

After Gary hung up, Deena looked back at Guttman. "Looks like our new suspect wasn't too fond of grapes after all."

＊ ＊ ＊

THAT ODOR AGAIN. JUST the smell of the gym caused Deena's calf muscles to tighten. She was like Pavlov's dog but with Bengay. The place was hopping. How did so many people have time to hang out at the gym in the middle of a workday?

Deena led Guttman to the check-in desk. The muscleman behind the counter wore a designer gray t-shirt with shredded holes across the chest. It read "Ripped."

Deena smiled. "Nice shirt. Ironic."

"Huh?" He stuck out his jaw like a caveman's.

"You know. *Ripped*. Like your shirt and your muscles. Right?"

He stared at her with his Cro-Magnon forehead slightly wrinkled. "I didn't iron it, if that's what you mean. It's a t-shirt."

Deena glanced at Guttman. Perhaps he could translate.

He tried to sound casual, which was not easy for the stressed-out detective. "We're looking for Layla Baxter. Know where we can find her?"

Cro-Magnon managed to cock his head without moving his bulging neck. "She works in the spa over there."

"Thanks, dude," Deena offered. "Maybe you can find a good tailor to sew that up." She walked off before witnessing what she imagined was a confused hulk who hadn't yet mastered language.

As they crossed the great divide between the gym and the spa, Deena sucked in the cool, fresh scent of lavender. The trickling of a water fountain and soft string music made her want to slip into a warm bath. No one was at the counter, so she tinkled the small brass bell.

Layla Baxter floated around the corner, a warm smile frozen on her face. Her midnight-blue bodysuit was embellished with a rhinestone belt that accentuated her tiny waist.

Her dark hair was pulled high up in a ponytail like Cyndi Lauper used to wear.

Judging from the look on Guttman's face, the tightly wound detective had turned into a puddle of goo.

"Hi," he said, like a thirteen-year-old boy looking at his first set of ta-tas.

"Hello. How can I help you?" The words came out of her mouth like honey on a biscuit. She hadn't even acknowledged Deena.

Deena broke the spell. "Howdy, Layla. How's it hangin'?"

Layla turned to Deena. "Oh, hi again, Mrs. Sharpe. I didn't expect to see you here."

Deena stiffened. "What do you mean? I work out. Sometimes."

"I just meant that the last time I saw you was at the winery. Now you're here."

"Oh. I see what you mean." Deena looked back at Guttman, who still had a goofy schoolboy grin. "This is Detective Guttman. We wanted to ask you a few questions about Andrew Granger."

"A detective?" Her dark eyes narrowed. "Now? I just started this job. I don't know if I can—"

"It will only take a few minutes." Guttman was back. "Is there somewhere more private we could talk?"

Layla glanced up at the clock. "I guess I could spare a few minutes." They followed her back to a small, sparsely furnished office. "I told Officer Hitchcock everything I know about Drew's death. What else do you want to know?"

Guttman took out a pad and pen.

Deena did the same. "By the way, I'm a reporter for the *Tribune*. Anything you say can and will...uh...be used in the newspaper." She made a mental note to work on a better intro line.

Guttman slapped on his stern investigator face. "What was your relationship to Andrew Granger?"

"He was my employer. I worked as a bookkeeper at Granger's Grapes."

He made a note. "Is that all?"

"You mean was I banging the boss?" She raised a perfectly plucked eyebrow. "Not hardly. I have a boyfriend. He's the jealous type."

Deena wasn't satisfied that this workout wonder woman was all she professed to be. Something about her was too perfect. "That doesn't mean you couldn't have been fiddling around on more than one violin."

Guttman shot Deena an odd glance.

"You know what I mean," she said to Layla.

"I'm very loyal. One man. At least only one at a time, that is." She winked at Guttman.

He cleared his throat. "Did Mr. Granger ever flirt with you? Could he have in any way assumed there was a relationship between you two? Perhaps only in his imagination?"

Deena wondered if Guttman was speaking from experience.

Again with the sultry smile. Layla practically purred. "Detective, I'm sure there are many men who have imagined having a relationship with me. But I can assure you, Drew wasn't one of them. If anything, he was more like a brother."

Guttman didn't bite this time. He spoke in his sternest Joe Friday tone. "Where were you on the night of the murder?"

Unfazed, Layla met his stare with her own. "I was here from six until about nine o'clock. I teach yoga. I had two classes back-to-back."

"Any witnesses who can verify that?" Guttman asked.

"Yeah. About forty of them. Maybe more. People in the gym tend to notice me." She smirked this time.

The door opened, and Marcus, the Treadmill Torturer from Deena's previous visit, burst in. "Is this guy bothering you?"

"A little," Layla said calmly.

That's when Deena noticed Layla was holding a cell phone in her lap. She must have sent out a bat signal.

Then Marcus turned to Deena. "Hey, aren't you the woman who almost passed out on the treadmill the other day? You're Gary's old lady."

Ouch. That stung. "This is Detective Guttman from the Maycroft Police Department."

Guttman rose from his seat and attempted to puff out his chest. At fifty pounds lighter than Marcus, the intimidation factor flew out the window.

Marcus did that side-to-side muscle bulge with his chest. "What do you want with my girlfriend, mister?"

"Just want to ask her a few questions about her boss's murder. Seems kind of fishy that she left her job there to come work here so soon after someone put a bullet in his head, don't you think?"

Marcus took a step forward. "No, I don't think."

"That's not surprising." Guttman pulled back his jacket and put his hand on his narrow hip, revealing his weapon and badge.

"Look, pretty boy, you may have a gun, but my guns are bigger and just as deadly." He curled up his arm to show off a bulging bicep.

"Are you threatening me?" Guttman put his hand on his revolver.

Deena stepped between the two men. "Come on, fellas. Let's not make a mountain out of a molehill." As she pulled Guttman into the hallway, he kept his eyes locked on Marcus's. "If we have any more questions, we'll be back."

Once they were safely outside in the parking lot, Guttman let out a deep breath. "I should arrest that guy."

"For what? Defending his girlfriend? You should be flattered that he felt threatened by you." Deena got in the car. "You heard him call you 'pretty boy.' You should take that as a compliment. At least he didn't refer to you as somebody's 'old lady.'"

Guttman started up the car and sped out of the parking lot.

Deena waited a few minutes for him to get his emotions under control. When he had slowed down and actually stopped at a yellow traffic light, she asked, "What is your take on Layla Baxter? Is she the jealous, jilted lover we are looking for?"

"Doesn't seem to be. Got any other leads?"

"Not yet. I'll call Vera again to see if she knows of anyone we might want to question." Deena's cell phone rang. "Hello?"

"Hi. This is Nina. I'm heading to Dallas in a while to catch a flight back to Nevada. Just thought I'd say goodbye."

"So soon? What about your brother's will?"

"Eric Lyons said it's going to take a while to sort things out. No reason to hang around here."

Deena looked at her watch. "I'm just a few blocks away from the Wisteria Inn. At least let me come by to properly see you off."

Nina agreed and mentioned that Mrs. Swanson had whipped up some delicious peanut butter and banana quesadillas. Deena's mouth watered just thinking about them.

Before getting into her own car, Deena promised to call Guttman as soon as she'd gotten in touch with Vera.

He seemed more than happy for her to take off as soon as they got back to the station. From what Deena could tell, he needed more time to heal his bruised ego.

Chapter 31

"I'M SURE GOING TO MISS this mild Texas weather," Nina said as she sat across from Deena in Mrs. Swanson's kitchen, sipping hot tea. "Where I live in the mountains, there's already been five inches of snow."

Mrs. Swanson's round body and warm smile moved around the kitchen with surprising quickness for someone her size. She was delighted to be serving another guest. "Coffee or tea?" she asked Deena.

"Whatever's easiest."

"I know," she said and snapped her fingers. "I'll make some of my famous hot chocolate you like so much. I remember the way you slurped it down and gobbled up those muffins when I served it at the church's Christmas luncheon." She fluttered about the kitchen like a busy bee.

Nina grinned and added warm honey to the already rich quesadillas. "I bet I've gained ten pounds since I've been here."

Deena tried to eat slowly now that she knew she had a reputation as a slurper and a gobbler. Still, she couldn't resist Mrs. Swanson's home cooking. "What are your plans now?"

"I've made a decision. I'm filing for divorce from Woody Davenport and taking back my last name. I waited too long to

197

reconcile with my brother and father, but I want to carry on the Granger name."

"Does that mean I should call you Edwina?" Deena licked honey from her fingers.

"Heavens, no. I've always hated that name."

"I think that's wonderful. It's about time you moved on. Will you be moving back to Maycroft after things have settled down?"

"Absolutely not," she said. "Nothing personal, but I love my job at the boys ranch. It's the first time I've found true purpose in my life. I can't wait to get back there."

Deena nodded. "But what about the family business? I mean, we still don't know what happened to Drew." She glanced sideways at Mrs. Swanson, not knowing how much she should say in front of her.

Nina picked up on the cue. "Oh, don't worry about Norma. I've told her every ugly detail."

Norma Swanson's ears perked up. She stirred the saucepan as she spoke. "Plus, I've been reading about the case in the newspaper. Will you put my name in one of your articles? After all, I was hosting the 'real' Nina Davenport. Don't think everyone in the Bluebonnet Club isn't going to hear about it."

"No doubt." Deena was delighted to hear someone talking about her stories. "Just wait until tomorrow's edition. I've got all kinds of new details to share."

Nina sat back. "Do you really think Allison killed my brother? I'd hate to think his life was cut short by someone he cared about."

"No, and I don't think the police do either. Right now, they're looking for a mistress or old girlfriend. You wouldn't happen to know anyone, would you?"

"Not hardly. Besides the obvious lack of contact, I can't remember Drew even looking at another woman before Allison."

Mrs. Swanson served the hot chocolate with miniature marshmallows and two pieces of graham crackers. "There you go, dear. I call it S'mores in a Cup."

The rich chocolate aroma filled Deena's senses. "Do you mix dark *and* milk chocolate in this recipe? I also smell a hint of almond bark. Is that what makes it so rich?"

"Why, yes!" Norma Swanson beamed. "You're the first person who ever noticed."

Deena took a gulp of the warm brew, quickly wiping away the marshmallow mustache. "Take that, Lonnie Fisher! I told him I knew my chocolate."

Nina glanced at her watch. "I wish I didn't have to leave so soon, but you know how Dallas traffic is." She stood up. "Thank you for everything, Norma. I promise I'll stay here again if I have to come back."

"*If*," Deena said. "Don't you mean *when* you come back? If you inherit the winery, there will be a lot to take care of, right?"

"We'll see. I'm trying not to live that far in the future anymore. I want to live in the present and see what tomorrow holds when it gets here." Nina gave Norma a big hug and picked up her bag.

Deena followed her outside to the car. "You have my number. Call if you need anything."

"I will," Nina said as she hugged Deena's neck. "I'll be following the news on the *Tribune*'s website." She got in the car and rolled down the window. "You know, this trip has been very enlightening. Even though my brother is gone, I feel like being back in this town helped me to understand him a little bit better."

"I'm glad." Deena stepped back from the car.

As Nina started to roll up the window, she stopped. "You know, until he married Allison, I always assumed my brother was gay." Then she drove off, leaving Deena to gobble down this new bit of information.

* * *

HOW COULD NINA THINK her brother was gay? After all, he had been happily married. Well, maybe not happily. There was the mysterious "queen" they were searching for.

Queen?

Deena pictured the two photographs that had been prominently displayed in Drew's office. One was of him and Allison. The other...

Oh my gosh! She ran back inside to grab her handbag. "Norma, I have to go. Something's come up." Before the woman could respond, Deena was out the door and racing toward the police station.

It had been Lonnie Fisher all along. How had she missed the signs? The gold ring on his right hand. His flimsy alibi about going to Dallas and missing his usual Thursday night card game at Drew's house.

And the note. No wonder Lonnie had it. Drew must have left it for him at the winery on the day he died. Drew was breaking up with Lonnie because Allison told him he was about to become a father. That also explained his lack of interest in his bombshell bookkeeper.

Deena pulled into a visitor's spot at the police station and went in to see Guttman. In her head, she was writing the lead for her next story: "Winery Owner's Partner Arrested for Murder."

Chapter 32

DEENA CALLED DAN WHEN she got home and laid out all the details of the story. He told her he would be saving the entire front page for her. He'd send a photographer out to Granger's Grapes to get some shots.

Unfortunately, she'd have to change the story's lead. As it turned out, Layla wasn't the only one who had quit the business. According to Vera, Lonnie Fisher had turned in a brief resignation letter, cleared out his office, and hadn't been seen or heard from since the previous day. Guttman put an APB out for him.

News story, news story, Deena thought as she anxiously read over her notes. *Most important facts to least important.*

By this time, everything was on the record. She glanced down at Hurley, who was curled up under the last bit of sunlight streaming through the window of her home office. Gary had texted that he'd be late getting home. Actually, that was fine with Deena. She needed time to hash out her story.

But it was quiet, and for a moment she thought about poor Allison Granger. Regardless of her strained relationship with her husband, she had gone from married to widowed in the blink of an eye. Deena couldn't bear the thought of being alone without Gary. She wanted to call him. Should she warn him about Lonnie? No, by now Guttman would have sent an officer out to interview Vera again and everyone would be watching out for Lonnie. Guttman said Lonnie had probably run off to Mexico or South America by now.

As she settled in to concentrate on the story, the words began to flow like water from a fountain. Her fingers flew across the keyboard as she got into the zone. Like an athlete hyper focused on winning at any cost, the words came to her as though she'd written this story before. Maybe she had...in her mind, anyway.

About halfway through, she stopped to call Eric Lyons for a quote about Allison's arrest. Hopefully, the district attorney would drop the charges. Small towns didn't have the resources to try little indiscretions when a homicide case would soon be on the docket.

Lyons was out of the office, probably meeting with the DA. Deena left a message. As she hung up the phone, the sound of shattering glass made her jump and Hurley started barking.

"Gary?" The loud noise seemed to have come from the den. She got up from her chair just as Lonnie Fisher appeared in the doorway.

"Mrs. Sharpe, why don't you sit back down. I was hoping we could talk."

Deena clapped her hands, and Hurley jumped into her lap. She could feel the thumping of her heart against his body as she clutched him to her chest.

"This is a lovely room," Lonnie noted as though he had dropped by for a cup of tea.

"They're looking for you," Deena said. "The police." That's when she noticed the wine bottle in Lonnie's hand. It had been hidden at first behind his trench coat.

"That's not surprising. I knew it was just a matter of time." He uncorked the bottle and took a swig.

"Here to give me a wine tasting lesson?" She hoped her light tone would keep him calm.

"No, although you could definitely use it." Several drops of blood dripped from a small gash on his hand.

"You're bleeding. Let me get a bandage."

"I'll be fine. That little bit of blood will be nothing compared to..." He sank into the chair by the window, the one Gary always sat in when he came home to find Deena working.

She searched her brain for the location of her cell phone. She had left it in her handbag on the entry table when she came home. Maybe she could send a message on her computer. She glanced at the Word document on her screen. She tried keeping it casual. "Gary will be home soon."

"It'll take him a while to get here. Those auditors mean business." He took another drink. His eyes were bloodshot and his nose was red. He'd been drinking a long time.

Maybe Deena could use Hurley as cover and reach for the desk phone without him noticing. If he was this drunk, his reactions might be slowed. She lifted her hand slowly just as Hurley jumped to the floor.

"I can see you're nervous. Don't be. I'm not here to hurt you."

"No? Then do you mind if I make a call?"

That's when he pulled out a gun. "It's too late for that." He looked down at the pistol. "I bet you're wondering if this is the gun I used to shoot Drew."

She steadied her breath, hoping to buy some time. "It's not. The police have that one. It was left at the scene."

"Very good. It belonged to Drew. Although that stupid cop didn't even know that when he staged everything to look like a suicide. Imagine my surprise when I found out they'd closed the case. I was off the hook." There was the slightest hint of a smile on his face. "But then you wrote that article questioning the investigation and opened up the whole can of worms." He balanced the gun on one leg while he finished off the wine.

Deena glanced at the door. Could she make a run for it? She pictured herself trying to get away. How many steps would she take before hearing the gun blast? She froze.

"I had been ready to go to jail after it first happened," he continued. "I didn't want to live without Drew. But then everything went back to normal, and I thought that maybe life would go on as usual."

"Why did you show me the note? Drew wrote it to you, right?"

He shook his head slowly and stared into the rug. "That was a mistake. I thought it could pass for a suicide note. I guess you figured it out."

"It was Allison, actually. She thought 'my queen' was another woman."

He stiffened. "*Allison*. She didn't deserve him. She didn't even know who he was. He said he only married her to get his father off his back. Once they had married, his father turned over his company to Drew."

Deena muddled it over. "Are you saying Drew knew about the morality clause in his father's will the whole time? Is that why he ended the relationship with you?"

"Yes. He said he couldn't juggle Allison, a baby, and me for another two years. Once he turned thirty-five, he had been planning on getting a divorce. But Allison messed that up when she told him she was pregnant. Such a liar. He said he couldn't damage the company's reputation by leaving her right after having the baby. She had ruined everything."

Deena heard herself ask, "So why didn't you kill Allison instead of Drew?"

He leaned forward in the chair. "You think I meant to kill Drew? You think I went over there to shoot the only man I ever loved?" He picked up the gun and waved it toward her. "I used my key. I went in. He was asleep on the bed. I knew he kept a pistol in the nightstand. I just watched him for a while." Lonnie was crying now.

Should she make a move?

He wiped his eyes. "I couldn't let her have him. Not after all we'd been through." Jumping from his chair, he came toward Deena. "That's why I'm here. I want you to put that in your story."

Deena's breath caught in her throat as she rolled her chair closer to the keyboard.

"Not on the computer! Use paper!"

He was more agitated now. He leaned over the desk. "I want you to tell everyone that he never loved Allison. He loved me. I didn't intend to kill him. I just lost it."

Deena's hands trembled as she tried to write down what he was saying. The pencil lead broke.

Lonnie grabbed a pen from her desk and shoved it at her, still holding the gun just a few feet from her face. It was the pen she had taken from Dan's office. "Read it back!"

Her voice shook. "Drew never loved Allison. He loved you. You shot him as an act of passion."

He nodded. "Act of passion. I like that."

The hum of the garage door drew their attention.

"Gary," she said softly.

"Make sure you print that," Lonnie ordered and took a few steps back. "And tell Gary I'm sorry." Then he ran out of the office and turned in the direction of the back door.

Deena rushed to the front of the house to meet Gary.

He took one look at her face. "What's wrong?"

That's when they heard the gunshot. The police found Lonnie's body floating in the swimming pool.

Chapter 33

HIS HAND TREMBLED EVER so slightly as he picked up the pen to sign on the line next to the red *X* on the final document. Was it fear or excitement causing the tremor? The small group who had gathered for the occasion waited in anticipation.

Deena put her hand on Gary's arm. "Wait." She dug in her handbag, then pulled out her "lucky" pen. "Here, use mine. It's the one I got from Dan and used to sign my contract with the *Tribune*. Hopefully, it will be lucky for you, too."

Gary took it and wrote his name on the final page of the document.

His friend Scott slapped him on the back. "Congratulations, partner, we are now the proud owners of our very own financial services agency."

"This deserves a toast," Jake, the loan officer, said. "Too bad we don't have any champagne."

Gary smiled and handed Deena back the pen. "Who needs champagne. I've got a case of some of the finest Texas wine you'll ever taste."

Deena smiled as her husband and his new partner shook hands and asked questions of the bank's assistant manager. For the first time since the tragedy of Lonnie Fisher's confession and suicide, she felt a sense of contentment. Her stories in the *Tribune* had garnered a lot of attention and had even been picked up by the wire services and run statewide. Dan and Lloyd Pryor had immediately offered her a contract and a generous salary, considering she would only be working part-time.

Deena kissed Gary on the cheek and then whispered in his ear, "No regrets about not buying in to the winery?"

"None whatsoever. I can't wait to move into our new office space. You know how much I'd have missed my suits and ties."

The frumpy woman sitting next to them overheard the comment and spoke up. "By the way, Mr. Sharpe, I don't mind picking up your dry cleaning on my way to work. Yours either, Mr. Myers."

Gary grinned and shook his head. "You're my secretary, Vera, not my wife."

Deena put her arm through Gary's. "That's right. He's already got one of those. And she couldn't be more proud of her husband today."

Over the chatter and shuffling of paperwork and chairs, Deena heard the ringing of her cell phone and pulled it out of her handbag. It was Dan. "Hello?"

"Sorry to bother you today, cutie, but I need you to come in to the office. I know you're busy, but it looks like we have another big story to cover."

Epilogue

LONNIE FISHER'S PARENTS held a small graveside service for Lonnie in Dallas. Vera Clausen and a few of the men who had worked at the winery attended. Gary and Deena went, too, although Deena told Dan she wouldn't be writing anything about it for the newspaper. It was enough that her story started the investigation into the murder in the first place. And her detailed account of Lonnie's suicide brought a close to the terrible saga.

She had struggled with her conscience when it came to including Lonnie's final message to Allison and the public. Lonnie had wanted everyone to know that Drew was a cheater who valued his business more than his wife and the child she claimed to be carrying.

Dan had drilled into Deena's head that the public had a right to know the facts. But she also remembered something Russell once told her. He said, "Sometimes the facts hurt more than they helped." In the end, she decided that as a reporter, she would always have to walk a fine line between justice and humanity.

After talking things over with Ian Davis, she was convinced that what Lonnie had said was hearsay and would not have been admissible in court. Therefore, she left the last part out of the story, that Lonnie said Drew had never really loved Allison. She knew all along she wouldn't print it, but getting the legal perspective made it easier.

As predicted, the district attorney dropped the charges against Allison since she was not involved in her husband's death. She got her husband's life insurance, the winery, and the money he had kept hidden from her in a secret savings account. But here's where it gets interesting.

Allison had no intention of running a winery or staying in the house she'd shared with a man who had been living a lie all those years. She sold the business—lock, stock, and wine barrel—to Owen Walsh for a fair price, although she did make one stipulation: he had to name one of his finest wines after the Sharpes. After all, she felt she owed them for all their help. And thus "Sharpe Sauvignon" sprang forth and went on the market in early summer.

In another surprise twist, Allison took some of the proceeds from the sale of the winery and made a sizable donation to the Boys Wilderness Ranch in Nevada. Nina was thrilled when the ceremony was held to present the check to the board of directors. Dr. Patton even dug into his own pocket to buy new chairs for their little conference room. The shabby card tables stayed, however.

Vera, as you know, went to work for Gary and Scott at their new agency. Owen Walsh had tried to get her to stay on at the winery, but Deena had convinced her husband that Vera would be a loyal employee. Besides, Deena knew she could "network" with Vera anytime she wanted to know the dirt going on behind the scenes at the office.

No charges were ever filed against Woody Davenport, Nina's ex-husband, although Detective Guttman threatened to throw him in jail if he did anything the slightest bit off the books in Maycroft again. After the divorce, Woody ran off to Houston with the cute redhead from Texas Tea & Tap. No one in Maycroft heard from him again.

Officer Larry Linndorf got fired, as expected. He served a few months in jail for covering up the murder. His lawyer got him a reduced sentence when he voluntarily agreed to give up his right to ever work in law enforcement again. Apparently, he moved up north and planned to try out for a minor league baseball team.

And as for Deena, that phone call she got at the bank from Dan turned out to be a doozy. It was a case like none she'd ever dealt with. But you'll have to wait for the next book if you want to know about that!

THE END

Works by Lisa B. Thomas

Maycroft Mysteries
Sharpe Image (Prequel Novella)
Sharpe Shooter
Sharpe Edge
Sharpe Mind
Sharpe Turn
Sharpe Point
Sharpe Cookie
Sharpe Note
Sharpe Wit
Sharpe Pain

Killer Shots Mysteries
Negative Exposure
Freeze Frame
Picture Imperfect
Ready to Snap

Beachside Books Magical Cozy Mysteries
(Co-written with Paula Lester)
Pasta, Pirates and Poison
Actors, Apples and Axes
Grits, Gamblers and Grudges
Candy, Carpenters and Candlesticks
Meatballs, Mistletoe and Murder
Honey, Hearts and Homicide

Visit lisabthomas.com for the most up-to-date book list.

Acknowledgements

THANKS TO ALL THE READERS who encourage me to keep writing. I feel your support every time I sit down to write.

A special thank you to my team of beta readers, editors, and designers. I can't wait to see what comes next.

Most of all, love and thanks to my husband for making it possible.

Made in the USA
Monee, IL
12 July 2020

36338936R00132